THE COWBOY HITCH

A CANYON SPRING NOVEL

S.M. WEST

KIMBERLY QUINN

Editor: Happily Editing Anns
Cover Design: KiWi Cover Design Co.

Welcome to Prospect, Montana, and the Kincaide family. Here's all the siblings and their stories to come. They are listed in order of their ages, not the release of their books:

One reckless, mind-blowing night with the sexiest man in town.
That's all I wanted. I got it and then some. Now I'm pregnant with my future at stake.

Ridge Kincaide.
Dominant.
Stubborn.
Sinfully possessive.

His family is small town royalty and I'm from the proverbial wrong side of the tracks.
We don't mix, and a baby is the last thing either of us needs.

But when I tell him the news, he claims to want us both.

Determined to win me over, he entices me with the idea of a home and life for us and our child.
Call it hormones, lust, or insanity, but my heart's all in—even if my head knows better.

No doubt Ridge could give me the family I've never had and always wanted.
But how can I trust the future he promises—or more importantly, him?

Life has taught me one sure thing. Nothing this good is ever real.
He's a Kincaide and bound to ruin me.

RIDGE

*L*acy Hallman, my one and only one-night stand, the only woman I can't get out of my head, and the one person I never expected to see tonight, watches me from across the room as I dance with my new fiancée.

My skin tingles and heats as her dark, hypnotic gaze tracks my every move. I still can't believe she's here. At my brother Brooks's very public, very crowded wedding. It's a gossip lover's dream venue, and practically everyone from the town of Prospect is here, waiting and watching for the next bit of scandal.

What the hell is she thinking?

"I have to admit," my fiancée, Chastity, drawls in my ear, "despite your crass demeanor, you're a much better dance partner than I expected." Her hands smooth over my shoulders, testing, maybe even teasing, and she presses closer, her pert tits brushing against my chest.

"Hmph." It's an unintelligible sound, but it's the best I

can do with all this anxiety—or is it excitement—humming through my veins.

It's not Chastity driving up my blood pressure, though. Sure, my wife-to-be is beautiful in the conventional sense. Willowy, blonde, and gleaming, she's upper-class style and grace personified. She's also my future, and should be the one capturing my attention, the one turning me on.

But she's not. We both know our marriage will be for appearances more than anything. Hell, I can barely stand to hold a conversation with her.

Instead, it's a woman from my recent past—a woman I spent just a single night with—who's got me hot and bothered.

Lacy.

Visions of her—wild, sweat-soaked, and coming hard—infiltrate my mind. I'll never forget the wicked, turned-on glint in her eyes, the way her hips rolled and chased after mine like she couldn't get enough. And the sounds she made, the way she moaned my name like a prayer.

Goddamn.

"Although, you're still carrying a lot of tension. You're a bit stiff," Chastity blathers, oblivious to my wandering mind and the irony of her words.

Despite my best efforts to stop it, all the blood in my body has rushed to my dick.

At thirty-five, you'd think I'd have better control over myself, and normally I would, but with Lacy still staring at me from across the room, it's impossible to even think straight. Especially when she's easily twice as gorgeous as I remember.

No, not just gorgeous. She's lush.

Lush as fucking hell.

Soft, full curves. Long, wild hair. Lips that, with just one look, you know can do some serious damage. Sensuous. Alluring. And...I need to get myself in check before this situation in my pants becomes embarrassing.

Chastity's grip on my arm turns claw-like. "Are you even listening to me?"

"What?"

"I suggested dance lessons. I think it would be good for you to practice before our wedding." Her eyes narrow, daring me to disagree.

She's already given me a lecture about my bad behavior once tonight, reminding me I'm not her only option for a husband. Under usual circumstances her warning wouldn't mean a thing. If it weren't for my family ranch, Canyon Spring, I wouldn't bother with marriage at all, but my controlling seat hinges on it.

Running the ranch is all I want—all I've got—and I'm willing to put up with a lot to secure it. Hell, I've already done a bunch of questionable shit to get my own way.

But dance lessons?

Fuck no. I'm not taking dance lessons or bowing to any of her other gentrification bullshit. I'm a rancher. A cowboy at heart. I do my dancing in the saddle. Or a bed.

Not on a parquet floor.

"We're practicing now, and that's the best you're going to get."

Her mouth pinches and nostrils flare, and it's all I can do not to walk away. To call off this sham of an engagement so I can stalk up to Lacy, grab a handful of her exquisite, silky hair, and kiss the hell out of her, right in front of everyone, including my soon-to-be bride.

Except, I can't. Even though she's a giant thorn in my side, I need Chastity.

Or more accurately, I need to marry her to keep my mother happy and fulfill the stipulations of my father's will.

Because none of my negotiating or scheming—and I've done a helluva lot of both—have gotten me around the terms of that goddamn will. Who'd have thought a piece of paper would have so much power to control, aggravate, and plain-old ruin lives.

Stupidly, I'd welcomed it. Pa named me head of our family ranch. Sure, it came with the condition of marriage to a woman of equal standing in the community and left the final say in Mama's hands, but I got what I wanted, the one thing I was promised, and that's all that mattered.

Only, Mama's grief has consumed her, clouding her judgment, and turning her from my biggest ally into a force of will to be reckoned with. The whole town knows Sage Kincaide is a powerful woman, but Mama's wielded that influence in ways they'd never imagine, and now she's using Pa's last wishes to regulate my life. Has been since the day he died.

Not just mine. Most of my eight siblings are under the thumb of our mother and a dead man too. Only two have escaped her recent guilt trips, manipulation, and outright blackmail—Clay, who high-tailed it out of Prospect at his first chance over a decade ago, and Brooks.

It took a lot for Brooks to give up his interest in running

Canyon Spring. As firstborn son, he seemed to think it was his birthright and didn't factor in my unrelenting drive and hunger for control. But after some of the shit Mama and I put him through, and after all the years of battling me for Pa's attention... Well, he put up a good fight, but I can't say I blame him for conceding.

At least he was brave enough to walk away when he'd finally had enough, and by marrying the girl next door today, he may have proven he's the smartest one of us all.

A sharp stab of jealousy twists my gut as I think of his happiness. The way he kissed his wife at the altar and how she threw her arms around his neck. They both fell into that kiss like it kept the world spinning. Neither concerned about appearances or how many eyes were on them. Together they radiate a kind of love I know I'll never have.

The kind of love that's irrelevant when I'll be head of Canyon Spring.

If marrying Chastity is what it takes to ease Mama's anguish and allow me to run things the way I see fit, then so be it.

Besides, if I play my cards right, I could end up running her family ranch as well. They're not nearly as big an operation, but it could still be a fun challenge to take them over. It would be a nice little reward for putting up with so much of her attitude.

The song ends, and—*thank you, Lord*—she leads me off the dance floor so she can take a break.

Except, now that I'm not turning in circles, I'm too restless, too agitated to sit and make nice. My eyes are glued to Lacy as she trails through the crowd, every step a seduction.

Not that I need to see her to know where she is. I'm so fucking aware of her, I can practically feel every move she makes.

"I'll be back in a minute."

"Where are you going?" Chastity levels me with an ice-cold glare.

How many years of her haughtiness will I endure before I learn to ignore it, ignore her, completely?

"Sweetheart, I'm about to become the head of a billion-dollar cattle operation. I'm always going somewhere or talking to someone. I'm at the beck and call of the business, not you. Sure hope you can learn to live with that."

Her eyes grow large, and she gives me a look I haven't seen from her before. It's like it turns her on to hear how important I am, and how many dollar signs come along with the Kincaide name.

But I'm not in the mood to entertain that. I can't even pretend to be attracted to her right now. Not when Lacy's only feet away, motioning me with her eyes to follow her outside.

"I said I'd be back, and I meant it. Okay?"

She nods, and I don't hesitate another second.

Tugging at the collar of my dress shirt, and not giving a shit about who might see the unfortunate tent in my pants, I stalk outside the barn, following the path I watched Lacy take only moments ago.

The lights and noise of the party fade and the night sky opens before me as I move toward the corral. Stars light my way, and the warm air feels like a cool balm, kissing my over-heated skin.

God, I love this land. The mood it sets, and the way, no matter how far I travel, I'm always somehow connected to it. It's a primitive feeling.

The same kind of feeling I get when I look at the woman waiting for me at the side of the corral.

Lacy.

Her arms are stretched over the top of the fence, one foot propped on the bottom post, and her delectable round ass pushed out as though to greet me. And all that hair...

Have I ever been turned on by a woman's hair before? I don't think so, but seeing Lacy's thick, dark waves blowing in the breeze has me picking up my pace.

By the time I finally reach her, I'm breathing so hard the sound fills my ears, competing with my banging heart for dominance.

But she doesn't seem to notice. Or at least, she doesn't seem to care. She stares into the fenced-off circle, her fingers twisting together anxiously, almost like she doesn't know I'm there.

"Surprised to see you here." *Fuck.* My voice is too rough. Too unforgiving. And even though the words are true, what I really want to say is how good it is to see her again. How much easier it is to breathe now that I'm here, with her.

Both her jaw and shoulders tense, and I can tell she wants to say something sassy to combat all my hard edges, but she doesn't.

She remains quiet, contemplative. Why the hell did she take the chance of coming here, knowing she likely wouldn't be welcome, if she's got nothing to say?

Unless maybe she wants to do something other than talk?

"Look." I inch forward, so close I could run my fingers through her glorious long locks.

It's tempting to do just that, but I keep my hands at my sides where they belong, respecting her space and trying hard not to completely lose my sanity. "It's not that I'm unhappy to see you, especially looking as fuck hot as you do. It's just bad timing."

Finally, she turns her deep gaze to me, the light of the moon reflecting in the dark pool of her eyes.

"Trust me, the timing's not great for me either." Her voice cracks, and now I can't help myself. I reach for her, my fingertips brushing down her arm before she pulls away.

"Ridge, I didn't come here to make problems for you, but I needed to see you and thought this would be the best way to do it, without raising too much suspicion."

"I take it you're not here for round two."

Her teeth graze her plump bottom lip, eyes become hooded, and she sways toward me before seeming to catch herself.

Damn. For a moment I thought she was going to fall into my arms and tell me she can't stop thinking about me, the same way I can't stop thinking about her.

But that's just fantasy. And even though I'd love nothing more than to feel her slick heat wrapped around my cock, to hear her chant my name while I plow into her from behind, to take her right here, right fucking now...I can't.

Because if I ever touch her again, ever truly feel her, I'd never want to stop. It's inexplicable and ridiculous, yet I know it's true. I'd want her bound to me. Submitting to me. Giving me every last piece of herself.

And I would lose myself in her. To her.

Then I'd lose Canyon Spring, and nothing's worth that risk.

No matter how desperate the craving. I've come too fucking far to give it up now. The empire my pa built is finally within reach, and I'll do whatever it takes to control it all 'til my dying day.

Even if it makes me ruthless and cruel.

Like father, like fucking son.

She holds her ground and my gaze, and despite the electric heat passing between us, her beautifully wild features remain guarded. Her head shakes subtly from side to side. Her sweet breath hits me in short, shallow bursts.

"Ridge..." God, I love the way she says my name. "I'm pregnant."

My body jolts and heart stutters, as the air trapped in my lungs claws and chokes its way out of me. "What?"

"Like I said, I didn't come here to make trouble. I'm not expecting anything. I don't expect anything at all. I just thought you should know."

That can't be...

I stare dumbfoundedly, her words twisting through my mind. My gaze drops to her full tits, and then lower to her belly, but she huffs a breath and crosses her arms over her chest, pulling my attention back to her face, her eyes, and the tears that are swimming in them.

"Are you sure? How do you know it's mine?"

Her gaze flashes with a fierceness so wild, so intent, it makes my dick hard all over again. It's the look she first gave me when we stumbled into bed together. A look that tells me I'm in a world of trouble, and *goddamn,* I'm gonna like it.

"It's yours—"

"I'm sorry," I interrupt, taking a step toward her, palms out, hoping like hell she doesn't retreat again. "It was just a gut-punch reaction. I'm not trying to insinuate—"

"I'm keeping it." Her chin quivers despite her ferocious determination.

"Okay." What the hell else am I supposed to say? I can't get my head around what the hell is happening.

How is it even possible?

"I know what you must think of me." Her voice drops to a near whisper, and her arms fall to her sides.

She sways closer, so close we're almost touching, and looks up at me with an expression so full of courage, it makes me feel weak.

"I know how this must look," she continues, "but I'm not a schemer, and I didn't get pregnant on purpose. I don't want anything from you."

"Lacy."

"No, I mean it. I only told you because it's the right thing to do." Her chest heaves and fists clench. "I don't need your money and I do not need you in my life to look after me. I'm nobody's burden, Ridge. Nobody's."

Burden? Why in the hell would she ever think that?

I open my mouth to argue, but she spins from me and takes off in a run.

"Lacy," I call, not even thinking about the boom of my voice, how far it might carry, or who might overhear. "Lacy."

But she doesn't stop. Fuck, she doesn't even slow. She

runs headlong into the darkness, leaving me staring after her like a goddamn fool, not knowing what I'm supposed to do next.

Am I supposed to carry on with things as planned? Can I marry Chastity and pretend like my life wasn't just irreparably changed by two little words?

2

———

LACY

My chest heaves and tears sting as I slide behind a tree. Gasping for breath, I bend at the waist and struggle for composure. I'm far enough away from the wedding reception, from Ridge, that no one will see me. Better yet, Ridge won't find me. That's if he even bothered to come after me.

More than likely, he's grateful I ran, and as much as I hate to admit it, I can't say I blame him. Our one night together was a reckless, irresponsible, albeit mind-blowing mistake. A mistake I'll never forget no matter how hard I try.

My hands rest on my still-flat stomach, and my head swims with images of our unborn child. The baby growing inside of me.

My child.

Ridge's child.

Dammit.

What on earth was I thinking when I jumped into bed

with the sexiest and cockiest—even if he has reason to be—man in town?

Oh, that's right...I wasn't thinking.

Now, I'll be reminded of the dangers and consequences of giving in to my basic instinct for the rest of my life. Just my luck, I got knocked up.

God, Lacy, could you be any more of a cliché?

I should have run the night he came into Oz's Club, especially when he started to pound back the whiskey. But nope, I stuck around. Couldn't help myself.

I'm a sucker for a man down on his luck, and this one was easy on the eyes. We may be from different worlds, but Ridge Kincaide caught my attention the first time I saw him in town. How old was I? Early teens, I guess.

He's always been hard to ignore, but when I was younger, boys were no use to me. All idiots and pains in the ass.

Still are most days.

Ugh. Since that night at Oz's, there have been too many times to count that I can feel his strong, calloused hands all over me, owning my body. The memory is fire. Vivid and hot.

He was all I craved.

Still do.

And it's only in those rare dark moments of weakness, like now, that I dare think it. Dare to think about Ridge and how I wish for a repeat.

Thoughts of his captivating blue eyes, wide open and locked with mine, and firm, full lips parted while he came, strip me bare every time.

There was something about him watching me as he came

undone...the hottest thing ever. It's as if he gave something to me that no man ever has.

A piece of him at his most vulnerable and most euphoric and I can't shake the feeling that was a first for him. He's never let anyone see him like that before.

I can't do this and not here with the Kincaides crawling all over the place. I wipe my face, hoping to erase any sign of my crying. Travis will go berserk—like he needs an excuse— if he thinks Ridge Kincaide or any of them made me cry.

Stepping from the shadow of the tree, the outline of my brother's head and broad shoulders fills one side of the truck cab. He rakes a hand through his mop of dark hair, and pride swells within my chest. I'm proud he kept his word and stayed put.

When I told him about the pregnancy, I was never more ashamed in my life, and that's saying something given our parents.

The baby wasn't the problem, even though unplanned and the added burden of another mouth to feed. No, my humiliation was in coming clean about the baby daddy.

I might as well have told him it was Satan himself. Travis isn't a religious man, but the Kincaides run this town and haven't made it easy for folks like us to make a decent living.

He'd fought me tooth and nail, insisting Ridge didn't deserve to know about the baby, fearing how worthless I'd feel next to the likes of the Kincaides and the other towns-people here tonight.

Travis is all I have. We have each other and it's always been like that. I can't remember a time when we weren't on our own, fending for ourselves.

With the town drug dealers for parents, we never had much of a family unit. Mom and Dad were either dealing or holed up in our piece of trash trailer, riding their latest high.

You see, unlike smart drug dealers—if there's such a thing—Otis and Arlene Hallman like to sample their product. A little too much. And their addiction and stupidity make it super easy for their suppliers to control them.

Our parents may deal the drugs, but we have always been dirt poor. Every dime they ever make goes back into their bloodstreams. Now being poor isn't a crime, but in this town it might as well be.

Travis and I had to beg, borrow, and steal to get by. During my childhood, not a week went by where we didn't spend our days and nights trolling trash cans and dumpster diving for food. Anything to fill our bellies. Anything to keep the ache of starvation at bay.

I swing open the passenger door of the cab and hop in, slamming the truck door for good measure.

"It's done." My elbow rests at the base of the passenger side window, fingers combing into my wild head of hair.

I squeeze my eyes shut, willing Ridge Kincaide to get the hell out of my head.

"And?" Travis starts the truck but doesn't put it into gear.

The oppressive weight of his expectant stare causes me to boldly turn to face him. I'm grateful for the twilight so I can hardly make out his disappointment. Or maybe it's mine, staring back at me like a mirror.

Darkness chases the pinky-purplish light painted across the sky. Full darkness will soon descend upon us and allow me to hide my raging emotions without scrutiny or questions.

"Is he gonna do right by you?"

"Do right? This isn't the 1900s." I snort. "What are you talking about? He isn't going to marry me, and I wouldn't agree to it if he tried, so don't even go there."

I jab a finger at him, and the bastard has the balls to laugh, shoulders shaking as he lays the back of his head on the seat rest.

This isn't funny, but I smile, nonetheless. If anyone can make me laugh at the disaster of my life, it's my brother.

"Shit, nah. You don't want to be saddled with the likes of the Kincaides, no matter if they're richer than God." He spins his upper body in my direction, bringing his face close to mine. "But he needs to pay your bills. Make sure you have what you need to take care of the baby."

Travis is no longer joking.

His tone is now a deep rumble, serrated and ready to cut. And only because he's so close, I don't miss the tic of the muscle in his jaw. He's strung tight and unable to hide how he hates this as much as I do.

"I didn't give him a chance to talk about any of that." Unable to look him in the eye when I tell him how much of a coward I was, I face forward and cross my arms over my chest. "I ran. I couldn't bear to hear him tell me to get rid of it. Not going to happen."

This baby wasn't planned but it's mine, and I can't walk away from him or her.

"There's no fucking way he's telling you what to do. Not

now, not ever." His hatred eats the air in the truck, and I inhale the little that's left.

He hates who we are, where we come from, and I feel the same way. But he also hates those who think they are better than we are, have more than we do.

"That's for sure."

"So now what?" His fingers tap on the steering wheel as we both stare at the glowing lights coming from the wedding reception.

Carrie Underwood's twangy lament filters through the air, mixing with laughter and hollering.

"Did he say anything of use?" His question is halfhearted. He's as done with this conversation as I am.

"No. Not really." I could defend Ridge and explain how he must be shocked, mind reeling with the news.

It took me several days to wrap my head around what a baby meant, especially since I was eight weeks along at the time.

Some might find it hard to believe that it took me that long to notice I was not only late but had also missed a period the month before. Although, being late wasn't that unusual. For most of my twenty-nine years, I've never had regular periods.

But Travis doesn't want to hear any excuses that benefit Ridge.

"When he comes around—because he's gonna once this sinks in—you tell him he's having a kid and he doesn't have a say in anything."

"I didn't give him much of a choice. I'm having the baby."

"What are you gonna do?"

"I don't know. I won't be able to work at Oz's once I start showing."

"You tell him yet?" His features are hard to read in the darkness, but his voice says it all.

Oz, my boss and owner of a strip club on the outskirts of town, won't be pleased. I'm the best bartender he has. And truthfully, he's more a father figure than a boss.

"Not yet. But soon. And without a job, I'll have to give up the apartment. Can I stay with you?" I'll need to save every penny, and staying rent free with my brother will help.

"You don't need to ask. Of course. This fucker better help you." He juts his chin in the direction of the highfalutin reception. "He has no choice. He's gotta help out his baby mama."

"Don't call me that, asshole." I punch him in the arm, and he flinches, yelping like a baby and rubbing at his bicep.

"That hurt."

"That was the point."

Still nursing his arm, he growls, "I don't know why the fuck you got into bed with that asshole."

"Okay, Travis. Not helping."

"Fine."

"What's done is done. It was a moment of weakness." How many times have I said that since falling into bed with Ridge?

I'm not a weak person.

"I said fine. Enough. I don't want to hear any more. The thought of you with that." He makes another gesture in the direction of the reception. "I'm going to kick his ass."

"No, you aren't." I buckle my seat belt. "Drive. Let's get out of here."

"Don't need to tell me twice." He reverses the truck and squeals the tires on our exit.

What a child.

Underneath it all, he's still the boy with the weight of the world on his shoulders. He was my protector growing up and I was his. There's nothing my brother wouldn't do to make sure I was taken care of. And the trade-off was huge. Among other things, Travis never got to be just a boy. A kid.

He guns the engine and I grit my teeth, holding back my curse or the urge to tell him to slow down. There's no point. He'll do the opposite if I say a word.

He needs to get his anger and frustration out of his system, and in the meantime, I grip the handle and hope he doesn't get pulled over for speeding.

There was a time I feared he might follow in our parents' footsteps. Prospect is riddled with judgmental residents. They make it hard to forget where you come from or reinvent yourself.

I should know, I've been trying my entire life. And so has Travis.

My brother is a natural with cars and wanted to open his own garage. He's got no formal training, but so far there's been nothing he can't fix. Once he got it in his head, he saved for school, taking business management courses online at night, and putting whatever was left away so he could get a place to set up shop.

In the end it didn't happen. Every bit of property in town

he wanted to lease, or buy outright with the help of a bank loan, which he qualified for, was met with opposition.

Obstacles everywhere.

The likes of Sage Kincaide and her cronies got in the way. They didn't think someone as dirty or lowly as Travis Hallman should run a business. Who did he think he was?

But Travis is a tenacious bastard. He didn't give up, and eventually, his dreams were close to coming true. He finally found someone who would sell to him. It was the perfect spot on the corner of Main Street.

Mr. Mueller, in his eighties with stage four pancreatic cancer, had first refused to sell his garage to my brother. And then, perhaps because he was dying or he was fed up with kowtowing to the powers that be in Prospect, old man Mueller changed his mind and agreed to Travis's terms.

He had nothing to lose, or so he thought, as he said to my brother. Until one night, before the paperwork was signed, his garage went up in flames and along with it went Travis's dream.

Now my brother works in the rebuilt garage, only it's owned by someone of Sage Kincaide's choosing. He's the head mechanic and the best in a fifty-mile radius. Folks from Helena will make the drive to Prospect if the job's a tricky one, knowing Travis is their man. He's thought about leaving. He could, but he won't. He refuses to be run out of town.

Me? All I think about is leaving, but who knows now.

Shoot. What have I done?

I can only imagine how Sage Kincaide will react when she hears she's going to be a grandmother.

3

RIDGE

Mack parks his new truck alongside mine, the chrome detail reflecting like a disco ball in the afternoon sun. It's an impressive and wildly expensive vehicle, and other than its size, doesn't suit him one bit.

I watch from my spot in the dugout as my best friend since childhood slides from behind the wheel with ease, then strides purposefully across the field toward me.

Mackenzie Mitchell is built more like a linebacker than a cowboy, although, you'd never know it from the almost graceful way he moves. The man can rope a calf faster than anyone I know, and makes it look like he's performing a damn ballet.

Still, from this angle, he looks like a giant. Or a redheaded grizzly bear.

How in the hell does he tolerate a full beard in this heat?

"Did you call me here to revisit the dreams of our wasted

youth?" The bench groans under our combined weight as he takes a seat beside me.

Together, we look out at the chalk-lined dirt of the Prospect High baseball diamond, the manicured lawn of the outfield, and the weathered bleachers that stretch to meet the bright blue sky. This is the place where, when we weren't busy working on a ranch, we spent all our spare time as kids.

He's not far off when he calls it a dream. I was the star player of our high school baseball team, the Miners. I wasn't always the fastest on the field, but as starting pitcher in our senior year, I led us to an undefeated state championship and was named MVP.

When I left this town on a baseball scholarship with UT Austin, I thought I'd make it big. Fuck, I almost did.

A career in the majors was just a signature away.

But of course, dreams like that require sacrifice and commitment, and I was already indentured to Canyon Spring Ranch. I'd foolishly believed I could have both. Thought Pa might be proud I'd made something of myself, on my own. But I was wrong.

Dreams like that—dreams that grow beyond the family, beyond Canyon Spring—were never an option.

This place reminds me of all the things in life I could've had if I weren't Devlin and Sage Kincaide's son.

"Nah. I'm not looking to rehash the glory days." I prop my booted foot on the dugout wall in front of us. "Just needed a quiet place to talk. The team has an away game today. I knew there'd be no one here."

"Must be important if you're pulling me away from work

on *your* ranch. What's going on?" His tone is casual, but I feel the concern lacing his words.

Like always, Mack senses when I'm troubled, and he's going to open his big teddy bear heart and do whatever he can to help me fix it. The man may be a solid wall of muscle on the outside, but on the inside he's just a big ol' roll of dough. We're such opposites, it's a wonder he ever became my friend, let alone the closest person in my life.

We got into a lot of shit together in the past—alcohol, teenage pranks, and girls were usually involved. But it was always my idea. I'd be the one dragging him down into trouble. Mack was always the one to pull us out.

Sure, I was the one who convinced Pa to hire him on as a hand after his parents lost their ranch, but that just gave me an excuse to boss him around and tease him about it after.

If he wasn't one of the nicest guys on the planet, he'd have probably told me to go to hell a long time ago. Or kicked my ass for being such an obnoxious prick.

Right now, I'm grateful he's not an asshole like me. "I don't even know where to start," I tell him.

"Start at the beginning. Just lay it out as it's in your head."

I let out a frustrated sigh, running my fingers through my close-cropped hair. "That's the problem. My head's all over the goddamn place. I just know I fucked up and I don't know what to do about it. I hate feeling like things are out of my control."

"You make it sound like that's something new." His mouth tips up to a teasing grin.

"Shut up, asshole. I'm serious."

"Sorry," he says through a light chuckle. "Just trying to

lighten the mood. Is it about the ranch? You having second thoughts about Chastity?"

Hell, I've barely thought of the ranch or my fiancée in the past three days.

After talking to Lacy, I'd gone back to the party, shell-shocked and disheveled, to find Chastity deep in conversation with Mama. It was easy to ignore her since she'd stopped riding my ass about my behavior. She was still starstruck, with dollar signs in her eyes and wedding plans filling her head.

I took her home in near silence that night and haven't seen or spoken to her since.

As for the ranch—well, the day-to-day practically runs itself, thanks to Mack and the people we have working for us. They don't need me watching over their shoulders all the time.

"I got someone pregnant," I blurt, but feel no better for having it out in the open. Instead, the words hang in the air like a heavy cloud, casting a dark shadow over this gorgeous day.

Mack sputters, "How?"

Is he laughing at me or choking on my admission? Not sure I care, but I'm about ready to hand him his ass if he can't pull himself together.

"How in the hell do you think? I know you've been hard up since Rayna dumped you, but you do remember how sex works, right? It's biology one-oh-fucking-one."

"Real nice." He stands, kicking a rock at his feet, and turns to me with a scowl. "Bring my ex into it. Remind me of the most painful time of my life. That'll make you feel better, I'm sure."

"Shit, man." I stand beside him, still looking out to the field so I don't have to look him in the eye. *Goddamn, I really am an asshole.* "I'm sorry. I shouldn't have gone there. It's not an excuse, but I'm really messed up about this whole thing."

"Well, no kidding." His voice is gruff but forgiving. Only Mack would let me get away with trashing him about the woman who broke his heart, and then stick around to hear my woes.

"But my question stands," he continues. "How'd it happen? Last I looked you weren't in a relationship—and no, your fake-ass arrangement with Chastity does not count. I'm pretty sure you haven't touched her."

"Damn straight." We share a look. He knows Chastity won't let me in her bed before the wedding, and I wouldn't want to go there, regardless.

But God, how sad is that? The thought of sex with my fiancée is so unappealing even my friend knows I haven't fucked her.

Finally, I turn toward him, leaning my hip against the dugout wall, shaking my head in bewilderment. "I don't know how it happened. I mean, I'm not a complete idiot, we used protection. It was just one night. I never expected it to turn into trouble like this."

"Who is she?"

I close my eyes, but quickly open them again when flashes of dark, windswept hair and luscious curves assault my mind. "Lacy Hallman."

Mack lets out a whistle. "That is trouble."

My shoulders slump, bone-deep weariness pulling me down. "Thanks, man, you're really helping."

"Hate to ask." He pins me with a guilty stare. "But are you sure it's yours?"

"Don't go there." I stiffen before sagging back down to the bench. "I know her family doesn't have the best reputation, but she's not like that. She's not a scammer."

"You sure about that?" He looms over me with his jacked-up arms crossed over his stupidly wide chest. "You say it was one night. How well do you really know her?"

My stomach's suddenly in my throat. It's the same sensation you get when going over the top of a roller coaster. Only, right now, it feels more like someone's pushed me off a cliff.

"I wasn't sure at first. But she told me in no uncertain terms it's mine, and I don't know why...but I believe her."

Mack joins me on the bench again, eliminating the awkward height difference and making me feel like I'm not quite so alone. "Okay. But believe her or not, you're still going to ask for a paternity test, right?"

A dry, brittle breeze sweeps into the dugout, making my eyes sting and my throat feel like the goddamn Sahara. "I don't know. I don't think she wants to have anything to do with me."

"Oh, for fuck's sake. You are not this shortsighted."

"I wouldn't be so sure about that." I shake my head, hoping to dislodge the absolute chaos within it. "It's ludicrous, and if you tell another soul I will beat your ass, but I'm kind of hung up on her."

The mix of dry air, racing heart, and sinking stomach makes me feel like I'm going to be sick. "When she told me, I was shocked and couldn't quite believe it. Yet, at the same time...I don't know...there's just something about her. Something I want to hold on to. Only it's impossible, you know?"

"Nothing's impossible, especially if it's what you really want, but did you forget you're already engaged?"

"Of course not. How could I? But that hasn't stopped me from thinking about it...thinking about her. Lacy." I sigh heavily and swipe a hand over my face, hoping to scrub away some of the downright insanity circling my mind.

"Listen." Mack's tone is as cool as ever. "Maybe you're just questioning things because so much in your life is out of your control right now. It raises doubts you wouldn't otherwise have. Or"—he looks me in the eye, his expression grim—"maybe you're finally allowing yourself to consider things because the doubts were already there."

"Yeah, maybe. I'm not sure it matters, either way."

"So, what are you going to do?"

It's the same question I've been asking myself on repeat for the past three days. Still, I don't have an answer.

All I can think about is how brave and beautiful Lacy was when she held my gaze and told me the news. She didn't back down. Didn't beg or threaten. Just told me how it was— how it's going to be. She might not have said a lot, but she was clear. Her plans don't include me.

"What can I do? My future is Canyon Spring. It's the only thing I've ever been allowed to want. And I do—I want it. I've given up everything else for it. And it's not just duty or obligation or even some misguided vengeance against Pa."

I swallow hard, wishing I had something cool to wash down the lump of emotion suddenly lodged in my throat.

"The ranch, the land, and everything on it are as much a part of me as my flesh and blood. I don't know what I'd do without it."

"Yeah," Mack agrees with a sigh. "But if that baby's yours, it's your flesh and blood too. And if you don't take care of it now, there'll come a day when it'll come back to take care of you. One way or another."

His words are ominous, which, coming from someone like Mack, makes them doubly impactful. But they're true.

If there's anything Devlin Kincaide taught me, it's how to take care of my own—even if they don't appreciate it. Even if it's against their will. When it comes to the best interests of my family, I can be downright greedy when I want to be. Ruthless when I have to be.

But I'm no good to anyone if I'm not head of Canyon Spring Ranch. Without that controlling seat, this whole town sees me as just another spoiled rich boy with a big mouth and a bad temper. As it is, most of the respect I'm given is in memory of my pa. My family name can only get me so far, though. I've still got a lot of work to prove I'm worthy, and the only way that happens is if I'm running the show.

"I know. I want to do the right thing here, Mack." My throat is so tight, I can hardly get out the next words. "I'll ask for a paternity test. If it's mine, I'll arrange financial support."

"That's it? You don't want a relationship with your kid?"

"It's not about what I want. It's what has to happen. Besides, what kind of father could I possibly be? I'm just as bad as Devlin ever was, and that's no kind of life for a child."

The look on Mack's face is hard to read—the stoic bastard may be full of feelings, but good luck ever getting him to show them. Still, I get the sense he's not on board with my plan.

"I just need to get it all under control," I continue, trying to reassure myself as much as I'm hoping to persuade him. "Once I've got my shit in order, things will smooth back out."

"Sure." He nods, obviously still unconvinced. "Until your mother finds out."

4

LACY

The cowboy tips his dark stubbled chin at me as I place a cold beer in front of him. The whiff of hops, or maybe it's his cheap cologne, causes my stomach to revolt. My insides churn and I press my lips together.

His eyes widen at the panic on my face as I dash from behind the bar. The urge to vomit barrels up my throat like a freight train without brakes.

Luckily, it's late morning and Oz's isn't anywhere near busy, with only the usual drunks and a few stragglers sprinkled throughout the club. I make it to the washroom in time, keeping my breakfast from hitting anywhere but the toilet bowl.

On my knees, I spill my stomach, and the stall door rocks back and forth behind me. The heat of someone at my back causes the hairs at my nape to stand, but I don't check who it is. I'm not done and heave once more, bringing up nothing but bile. My shaky hand tears off some toilet paper to wipe my mouth and I flush before getting to my feet.

Lynette stands outside the stall, smacking her strawberry Hubba Bubba with her hands on her bony hips. Concern with a hint of knowing colors her heavily made-up face. "How far along are you?"

"What are you talking about?"

"Let's try that again." She arches one perfectly shaped ginger eyebrow, twisting her bright red lips. "Answer me."

I try to push past her, but she mirrors my moves. "Lacy, don't even try to tell me otherwise. Take it from me. Three here." She points to her flat stomach where, in fact, she did carry three boys.

The woman's pushing forty but doesn't look a day over thirty and all her kids live with her mother. She may be good at conceiving but that's about it. As the oldest stripper, the only mothering she does is to the girls here at the club.

I'm not a stripper, not that there's anything wrong with it. It's an honest living and who am I to judge. While I'm as confident as the next, stripping's not for me.

Not that I have a problem baring skin if I want to. Just ask the boys at graduation. Skinny-dipping won me five hundred dollars.

Those jerks never dreamed I'd do it when I bet them. Yes, I was poor white trash who needed the money, but I never dated or put out. I was so damn virginal most gave up even trying.

"Lacy, honey, talk to me." Lynette's insistence drags me back to my present predicament.

Unfortunately, she considers herself in charge of everyone's business and that includes mine. "Fine. I'm almost ten weeks."

She moves out of my way so I can rinse my mouth, spitting several times before washing my hands. All the while, the sexy redhead studies me through the bathroom mirror.

"Don't tell Oz." I turn off the tap. "I'm telling him today."

"Who's the daddy? Do I know him?" She cocks a hip and plants her hands on her waist, narrowing her gaze at me. "Please don't tell me it's Gentry."

Spinning to face her, I smirk. I want to see her squirm, just a bit. Gentry's one of the bouncers. Nice guy. Hot if you like beefcakes, and it's no secret he has a thing for me. And in turn, Lynette has a thing for him. She's always got a thing for someone. Some days this place is a soap opera.

"No, it isn't."

"Then whose is it?" Now she's begging and when I walk by her, she grabs my shoulder. "Come on, Lacy, you can trust me."

I snort, but hold back the derisive comment prickling the tip of my tongue. Lynette never met a secret she could keep.

"Someone wanna tell me why my bar is fucking unsupervised?" Oz's tall lean frame eats up the doorway, and his Sam Elliot tone, that iconic timbre, causes both of us to straighten.

When not performing or working the floor, Lynette helps out with drinks and I'm on shift today. My ass should be behind the bar.

I slide past the woman, grimacing. "Shit, Oz, I'm sor—"

"Hold up. I wanna talk to you." One weathered finger points at me and I falter while his dark gaze shifts to Lynette.

"You, get out there and take care of Hank. Give him a shot of bourbon for the wait."

"All right, boss." She sashays past him, playfully swatting at his ass, and he mashes his lips together, unimpressed.

The door swings closed, and he stands there, all six foot two of him. He's in good shape for his age, broad and muscled, and back in the day he was a looker, not that he isn't now.

Oz is in his early sixties with a full head of hair, white as snow but so thick you want to run your hands through it, and his square jaw, strong nose, and deep-set brown eyes round out his handsome, rugged features.

"You got something to tell me?" He stares intently at me.

My mouth gapes and I want to demand answers. Who told him? But I know better.

I may not be showing—thank goodness, not yet—but there's no way he'd be as successful as he is, owning the only joint of this kind in the county, without being sharp as a whip and super perceptive. He has to be to hold his own with the wealthy, uppity bunch. He's figured out my current state all on his own.

"Um, yeah." I glance down at my fingers, stomach still unsettled, and I'm unsure how to fess up to something he's heard a million times before. Although I'm willing to bet he never imagined hearing it from me. "I'm pregnant."

His chin dips and he rests a hand on my shoulder. "How far along?"

"I'm almost at the end of the first trimester."

He nods. "You feeling okay?"

I nod, unable to find my tongue. Shame never gets easier

and he isn't even casting judgement. He isn't that kind of man.

"Good. What do you need?"

"Um, nothing for now. I'll work for as long as you'll have me."

A tender grin ghosts his lips. "Well, I can't have a pregnant woman behind the bar, although half these boys come in here for you."

I scoff and roll my eyes, tired of the same song and dance. Years ago, with my tail between my legs and behind Travis's back, I slunk in here, starving and broke, looking for a job. No matter how things look from the outside, this club is a haven for many women who are out of options or have no place to go.

One look and Oz asked if I'd strip. I said yes, but he could see it wasn't my thing. Without any discussion or fuss, he taught me to tend bar and claims that ever since, business has doubled whenever I'm slinging the drinks.

It's flattering even if there's isn't a lick of truth to it.

Fact is, Oz is the closest thing to a father I'll ever have. I'd trade my real one for him any day and that's why this is so hard. I don't want to disappoint him.

I was saving for a one-way ticket out of here, and he fully supported my goal. Even stepped in when Travis got mouthy, trying to dissuade me from leaving.

The baby changes everything.

I'm no longer going anywhere.

Like so many before me, my chances of something different—better than I have now—just got harder or maybe near impossible.

"I'll stay until I start showing. Maybe four, five months. Six if I'm lucky."

"That's unless you're willing to show off the belly. Bet I could bring in a crowd for that." He winks at his tasteless joke.

"Not a chance, perv." I hit his chest and he chuckles.

"No way I'd put you in that position. But I'll find you something to do that keeps you off your feet."

A warmth blooms in my chest at his generosity. "Okay. Sounds good. I can do that. Thank you."

"You can stay at the apartment for half the rent. It's the best I can do, kid." He also owns the building where I live and has helped me in more ways than I can count.

"Thanks, but I'll have to eventually leave. I need every penny I can save."

"Aww, shit, Lacy." A wrinkled hand threads his hair. "I wish I could help you out and waive the rent. The best I could swing is one month rent free, maybe two. Tops."

"No. No. I appreciate it, but you got to make a living too. I can stay with Travis. Let me take a look at things and figure out when I'm leaving." I squeeze the older man's arm and he gifts me another warm smile. "It's all good."

He can be one mean son of a bitch. There's many a rancher or passerby that won't step foot in this joint because they made the mistake of crossing Oz Barker. But underneath his gruff exterior and no-nonsense attitude is a big ol' gooey heart of gold.

"It ain't my business." He shifts from one foot to the other. "But who's the father?"

Dammit. Of all the things I'd hoped he wouldn't ask...

well, at least not today. There's no question I can trust Oz. Unlike Lynette, he'll take any of my secrets to his grave.

"Um..." I start to look away, but he pinches my chin, keeping my head in place. "Ridge Kincaide."

"Holy shit, woman." He tilts his head back, releasing his grip on me, and lets loose a belly laugh. "You sure know how to aim high."

My eyes bulge and I gawk, surprised at the insinuation, and my high-pitched voice doesn't hide my offense. "I didn't do it on purpose!"

"Not suggesting you did. Just saying, if you were looking to get yourself into a lifelong pickle with endless heartache... you hit the fucking jackpot."

"Yeah, thanks for telling me something I don't already know." My arms fold across my middle.

"You tell him?" He's suddenly serious and I nod, not wanting to get into this. "And what did the mean mother-fucker say?"

"Not much." I shrug. "I didn't give him a chance."

"Well, if he causes you any trouble, you come see me. I'm always looking for an opportunity to go toe to toe with a Kincaide." Sarcasm drips from his deep rumble. I bark out a laugh and he joins in as he holds the door open for me.

We saunter into the main area of the bar, greeted by the familiar twang of country music blasting from the stereo system. A few more people have come in since I ran into the washroom, including my best friend, Kelly.

"Hey, Lacy." She jumps off a stool and pulls me in for a hug. "Hi, Oz."

"K-girl." He winks and moseys past us toward the office.

"Hi, Kel. You're early. Doesn't your shift start at nine?" I slide behind the bar, and she settles back onto her seat.

"Yeah, but I thought I'd help Lynette." She leans in and cups a hand to one side of her mouth, lowering her voice. "Since you have your appointment."

I smile at her attempt to keep my pregnancy on the down-low. Next to Travis, and now Oz and Lynette, Kelly's the only other person I've told. Well, except for Ridge, obviously.

"Thank you. That's sweet of you. But honey, are you sure working the bar is the best way you can help?" I'm teasing but also dead serious.

She spills more drinks and breaks more glasses than anyone else when tending bar, which isn't often. Oz won't allow it. Kelly's a klutz. Can't help it, she comes by it honestly.

From as young as I can remember, the girl was always scraping, breaking, or bruising something. And at first, she tried to hide her daddy's beatings on her butterfingers or lack of coordination, but Travis was quick to figure out she was lying.

"Why you ungrateful girl." She slaps the bar top and her long, blonde hair sways from side to side. "I get up early, way before my time, to help my bestie and this is how you thank me? Givin' me sass?"

I giggle, grabbing her hand for a squeeze. "I'm sorry. I just wonder if Oz knows you're going to be on bar while I'm gone."

Today is my first doctor's appointment about the baby, and I'm grateful Kel's here to cover for me. She won't take a dime from me for the hours she covers my shift. The girl makes more than me on stage, and she also won't cry on Oz's shoulder. Sadly, there are girls who'd say yes to helping me, only to moan about it behind my back.

"All I can do is try my best. I mean, how hard can it be to pour a few drinks and bring the guys their beers?" She tosses her hair over her shoulder, glancing at the cowboy two stools down, and winks.

From a few feet away, a man growls and we both look in that direction. Travis. He's standing ramrod straight, angrier than a bull, and shooting daggers at Kelly.

"Oh, look who's here, the town grump." Kel throws her own verbal knife his way before turning her back to him.

She waves to the older cowboy still lusting after her like he's dying of thirst and she's the last drop of water on earth.

Kelly's a beautiful woman, inside and out, and without a doubt, the biggest draw in the club. She makes Oz a boatload of money. The girl's so popular she only works a few nights a week.

"Why don't you put some clothes on," Travis snarls at my best friend, and I push at him before he gets in her face.

"Not today. Let's go." I glare at him, making sure he understands. Then I glance back at my friend. "Thanks so much, Kel. I should be back in about an hour or so."

"No problem, and don't bother coming back. I've got you covered. I'll stay behind the bar until Roxy comes in. You take it easy."

Shocked, I open my mouth, ready to protest her sweet offer, but Kelly keeps talking. "And good riddance, Travis." She twists her lips and makes a childish face at him.

My dumbass brother does the same as I nudge him

toward the door. If we don't leave now, these two will be at each other's throats.

Suddenly, the queasiness is back, but it isn't morning sickness. I'm nervous about this appointment. I've no clue what it entails and all I want is for the baby to be healthy. For everything to be all right.

5

RIDGE

Chastity sweeps out from the Hidden Gem Salon in a flurry of bags and hairspray. She looks like she belongs in the Big Apple, instead of on Main Street in Prospect, Montana—or at least the TV version of New York, where everything's high-end, overdone glitz.

"Well?" She beams at me and does a little twirl. "How do I look?"

Honestly, she looks identical to how she did two hours ago, before she went in for what she called a *refresh*, but I'm not about to say that shit out loud.

Instead, I give her a curt nod. "You look real nice."

From her reaction, that was clearly not the answer she was looking for. Her mouth pinches and a fine line forms between her perfectly manicured eyebrows.

"Nice?" she mimics.

I hold back my sigh. "Yep. Real nice."

We stare each other down, neither of us giving in to the

other's silent demand, until it feels like we're both wilting a little under the midday sun.

I wish I'd worn my Stetson. When I decided to leave it at home, I thought it would be easier to put up with my brain getting a little baked than to listen to my uptight fiancée complain about my manners, but now I'm having some serious regrets about that choice.

How this woman grew up on a ranch is beyond me. She sees one speck of dirt, one sign of what she considers unrefined behavior, and she acts like the sky is falling.

Even Mama, with all her grandiose ideas of class and power, still understands the core values of what we do. Of who we are.

We may have gardeners, maids, and a world-class chef on staff—hell, we're even evolving with the times and moving forward on an environmental sustainability plan—but we're still cattle ranchers. Most everything about our business is done in the dirt, and some would consider it uncouth. Fuck, most of our money comes from all the filthy and underhanded deals my pa made. Deals Mama and I still honor and still make to this day.

More and more I'm realizing Chastity doesn't fit into that picture. If she had half a clue about some of the things I've done...the things I like to do...

"C'mon," I say, turning my back on her and shoving down my misery.

Happiness doesn't factor here. It can't. Not with Pa's will controlling my goddamn destiny, and Mama still determined to make his last wishes stick. Not if I want Canyon Spring Ranch.

"Don't want to keep Mama waiting. You know how much she values shit like punctuality."

Chastity doesn't argue, but from the punchy staccato of her heels against the sidewalk behind me, it's obvious she isn't thrilled with me. Or maybe it's my *colorful* language. Who the hell knows.

I'm torn between wanting to walk faster to leave her in my dust and turning 'round to apologize. Not that I'm at all sorry, but it'll sure make the rest of this afternoon easier if she thinks we're on the same page.

I ease my pace, ready to do some big-time fake groveling, when a couple on the other side of the street catches my attention. They're a good fifty feet or more away, and their backs are to me, but I'd know those curvy hips and the thick flow of sable hair anywhere. Lacy.

A jolt of lust—hot, heady, and demanding as fuck— rockets through my body at the sight of her. When the man she's with slings a possessive arm over her shoulders, another feeling altogether, something akin to jealous rage, rocks me to my core.

Who the hell is this guy? A boyfriend? A lover?

Lacy never mentioned having another man in her life. Not that there was much opportunity between hopping into bed together and our blowup over the impending outcome of that romp.

Still, she never acted like she was attached to someone. Hell, she said she didn't want to be a burden and I kind of assumed she meant to anyone. Not just me.

I watch as he pulls her a little closer, their dark heads

tilting toward one another, and she slides her arm around his waist.

My blood pressure spikes and my vision turns a little fuzzy.

I don't know who this chump is, but if he thinks he's going to sidle up on my woman and kid, he's going to be a dead man.

I spin back toward Chastity, who also looks ready to commit murder, only her animosity is all aimed at me.

Good. It'll make this next part all the easier.

"I've got something I need to take care of," I bark, leaving her no room to argue. "You should head to Walter's and secure our reservation. I'll meet you and Mama there when I'm done."

Her eyes narrow at me, but she doesn't say a word. She simply keeps on walking right past me, with her nose in the air and unmovable blonde bob shining in the sunlight.

I watch her walk into Walter's North Bistro—my heart banging like a jackhammer—before stalking across the street toward Lacy and the asshole who's still got his arm wrapped around her.

It doesn't take much for my long, heavy stride to eat up the sidewalk between us. It helps that they're only sauntering along. But seeing them relaxed—even thinking they might be happy together—pushes my anger up another notch. Especially when I realize where they're coming from.

Doc Anderson's office.

My stomach sinks, and a sick feeling joins my boiling rage, creating a cacophony of mixed sensations. I'm still sweating under the heat of the sun, but my skin prickles, and cold dread creeps up my spine.

Breathing feels like torture with the weight of anxiety crushing my lungs. "Lacy." Yet, I'm somehow still able to shout her name.

They both freeze, and then slowly—ever so fucking slowly—turn to me in tandem.

"What is going on here?" The words squeeze past my grinding teeth. "You're seeing the doctor with this guy? If it's for the baby, I should be with you. Me. Not this fool."

The look on her face is unreadable. Shock, maybe a hint of fear or perhaps simple embarrassment. Whatever that look is, she seems suddenly deflated, her casual happiness seeping out of her like air let out of a tractor tire.

With my focus zeroed in on her, I'm unprepared when the guy shoves forward, getting up in my face. "Stay the fuck away from her."

Wrong move, buddy.

My hands are already clenched to tight fists, and before I'm even conscious of it, my right hook is plowing into his face.

He staggers backward, caught off guard by the move, but has enough sense to raise his fists as blood trickles from the corner of his busted lip.

"What the hell, Ridge?" Lacy cries, scrambling to get between us.

She's gorgeous with her dark eyes wide, wild hair flying, and delicate cheeks flushed. I want to grab her, pull her to me, crush my mouth to hers, and claim her as mine.

Where the fuck these caveman urges have sprouted from

is beyond me. I've got no right to her, no goddamn claim to make. And even though it's not my first tussle this summer—my brother Brooks and I traded blows just a few blocks from here—I've sure as hell got no business attacking someone on a public street.

If Mama saw any of it, there'll be hell to pay.

Still, I can't calm the wave of emotion crashing inside me. "Who the fuck is this guy?"

The jackass wipes at his bleeding mouth and fakes a lunge for me. But Lacy's arm shoots out in front of him, as though it were a barricade that could hold him back.

"Don't you dare," she hisses.

I'm not a fool, and this guy's no slouch. He may be shorter than I am but he's also stockier, and I've no doubt if he wanted to make me hurt, there's not much Lacy could physically do to stop him.

Yet, she has.

He's still visibly agitated, but with her simple gesture and low-level threat, he backs off completely.

"I need a minute with him," she says.

The jackass doesn't respond, but she doesn't back down, silently communicating something to him in her weighted stare. Something he seems to understand.

If his growl is any indication, he doesn't like it, but he still gets it. "Fine. But if he says or does one thing to hurt you—"

"I'm not going to hurt her," I snarl.

"I wasn't talking to you, asshole." He points a finger at me, daring me with his eyes to make a move.

"Travis. Enough." Her tone is stern, but the edge of her

voice is tinted with weariness, making me worry I've taken this too far already.

Fuck, maybe this guy, *Travis*, is right—maybe I'm already hurting her without even knowing.

He gives another growl of frustration, but still does what she's asked, shaking his head as he paces away from us.

"I'm sorry—"

She whirls to me, cutting off my apology. "I don't know what the hell you're doing or who the hell you think you are, but you have no right to come up on us like that. Why would you hit my brother? You've got no right at all, Ridge Kincaide!"

Her brother. Travis Hallman. *Goddammit.*

"Shit, Lace...I know...I'm an asshole."

"Yes, you are." She crosses her arms, which I'm sure she does to make herself look tough, but only succeeds in plumping up her ample chest and making my cock take notice.

How in the world am I turned on right now?

Guess when it comes to this woman, it doesn't matter if we're lovin' or fightin', my body likes her all the same.

"I've got no excuse for it," I tell her, talking about hitting her brother, but maybe also the growing bulge in my pants. "I just saw you two together and not realizing who you were with...well, I guess it set something off in me."

Dark eyes bore into mine, and I have to drop my gaze to keep my head on straight.

"That makes no sense at all."

She's right, and I know it, but it doesn't change a damn thing. I still want to drag her out of here—away from her brother and the prying eyes of Main Street. I want to lock her up somewhere safe, somewhere we can be alone. Somewhere I can ravish her amazing body, and then maybe talk a spell before falling back into bed and doing it all over again.

"Is everything okay with the baby?" I ask, forcing my thoughts back to where they belong.

She sucks in a sharp breath like I've slapped her and takes a step back.

My eyes whip back to hers, concern radiating from every part of me. "God, Lacy, please tell me it's all good."

A subtle shake of her head has my insides crumbling, until she squeaks out, "It's fine. Everything is good."

I swipe my hand over my face, clearing away the sweat, and practically double over with relief.

It's the oddest damn thing because I never really pictured myself as a father. I mean, I always figured I might have to consider it someday, to continue the Kincaide family legacy and all, but it was never something I set my sights on. Maybe it's because, with eight siblings, the pressure to reproduce wasn't imminent.

I always thought, if it was meant to be, then it'd be.

But now that it's happening—now that the idea of fatherhood is breathing down my neck—I'm not as disassociated as I expected. In fact, part of me is ridiculously looking forward to it.

Only, that's the part of me that wants to believe I can have it all. The part of me that wants to pretend I can turn my back on all the bad shit I've done, all the ruthless things I'm going to do in the future, and just be a simple man. A cowboy and a dad.

It's the idealistic part of myself that says, "*Guess it was meant to fucking be, asshole.*"

Not knowing how to express any of this to Lacy, or if I should even try, I give her a tight smile and murmur, "Good. That's really good."

I feel a bit like an awkward schoolboy. Or a lame horse getting sent out to pasture. But what the hell am I supposed to do? How do I handle this situation now that I've fucked it all up?

I've got no time left to figure it out. Travis is back, and he's having none of my bullshit. I can see it in his glower. Not that I blame him.

"C'mon, we gotta go." His hand lands protectively on Lacy's shoulder, urging her away from me.

Nodding absently, she turns to leave.

"Wait," I blurt. "Can we talk sometime? For real?"

"You've wasted enough of her time." Travis scowls harder at me. "She's got nothing to say to you and doesn't need to hear any more lies from a Kincaide."

"Lacy?" I urge, hoping she at least stands up for herself, instead of letting her brother do it for her.

But she doesn't.

Instead, she jerks out of Travis's hold, turns her back on both of us, and walks away.

He points his finger in my face again. "Leave my sister the fuck alone, or next time I won't be so nice."

Not bothering with a reply, I stalk back across the street and straight into Walter's.

I understand his anger. If the tables were turned and he'd gotten one of my sisters pregnant, I wouldn't have bothered with a warning. I'd have pummeled him just for the sake of it. Still, if he thinks he's scared me off, he's sorely mistaken.

As I pull open the door to the fanciest restaurant in town, a blast of cool air hits me, along with the weighted realization of the decision I've made.

I'm not turning my back on Lacy or my kid.

With my chest tight and stomach aching, I step inside to find Mama's been watching from this side of the glassed-in foyer. *God, how much did she see?*

"What's going on, Ridge?" Her cool tone does nothing to hide her irritation. She props a hand on her trim hip and shoots me a look I'm sure is meant to intimidate. "Who is that trashy-looking woman you were talking with?"

Something inside me snaps.

I'm so done with this. Done with the lies. The games. I don't care how bereft she is after the death of my father, her attempts to browbeat me into submission end now. I'm not a pawn. And I'm tired of playing nice.

"You mean that smart, strong, all-natural beauty?" I snarl. "*She* is the future mother of my child. Congrats, Grandma."

6

LACY

*M*ean old Mrs. Stanton glowers at me from under the brim of her sun hat as I stomp across Main Street toward her. I've been walking around town, stuck in my head, trying to get my roiling emotions under control.

I'm only feet from where the overwhelming stench of testosterone made me sick while Ridge and Travis went head-to-head, acting like overbearing idiots. I had to get away from them, and luckily, enough time has passed that they're both gone. Good riddance.

Stuck in my thoughts, I nearly collide with the pious Edith Stanton, once my fifth-grade teacher and famous for whacking your hand with a ruler without provocation. Let's just say, I wasn't one of her favorites and to this day my left palm stings at the mere sight of her.

"Watch where you're going," she snaps, making a big show of cowering while stepping to one side like I'm some threat to her. *Please.*

"Excuse me," I mutter and quicken my pace.

It's hotter than hell today for September and I'm already fuming from the run-in with Ridge outside of the doctor's office two hours ago. I don't know who I'm madder at—Ridge or Travis. Dumbass hotheads.

It's bad enough growing up the town trash with everyone talking behind your back. But today is an all new low. Many townsfolk witnessed our tussle with the king, Ridge Kincaide. I can only imagine what the gossips will say.

"Did you see those nasty Hallmans trying to pickpocket Ridge Kincaide?"

Or maybe, "Travis, the big thug, beat him up and you know, that Lacy, the loose one, she threw herself at him."

Delirious laughter erupts as I imagine how ridiculous the stories will be that are sure to spread. At the same time, my stomach churns and emits a shocking rumble.

I'm hungry, a little lightheaded, and all too emotional. The appointment with Doctor Anderson went well. Tears welled at the corner of my eyes when he pointed to the tiny pea-size blob on the screen of the ultrasound.

And the *thumpity, thump* of the heartbeat had me a mess. Heck, even Travis cried. In that moment, stomach smeared with wet goo, both my brother and doctor staring down at me, nothing else mattered.

The baby made everything else seem unimportant. I'd thought about being a mother one day, and now it was closer than I'd ever dreamed. And as for Ridge, I hadn't thought of telling him about the appointment. Not out of spite or anything like that, but more because I told him the news over a week ago, and I've heard nothing from him. Not that I had expected to.

But when he'd asked about the baby...his interest was near palpable. His concern and then, dare I say, joy and relief were hard to miss in the smoothing of the tiny lines around his mouth and the spark lightening his blue eyes.

I blink and a hot, fat tear slides down my cheek. Damn. I'm one big ball of emotions.

Water and food, that's what I need. Mel's ice cream parlor is two doors down, and cool, creamy mint chocolate chip is calling my name.

Doctor Anderson's words filter through my mind from not even an hour ago. "You need to take care of yourself. Eat lots of vegetables, make healthy food choices, and get plenty of rest and fluids."

I don't suppose a double scoop counts as healthy. But wait, there's calcium in dairy. That has to be good for the baby, and there's protein. It's better than nothing and I can't continue walking around on an empty stomach.

I walk into the parlor and the cold air hits me as my phone buzzes with a text.

Kelly: Your jerk of a brother was just here looking for you. Are you okay?

I breathe in the delectable warm waffle cone aroma and step to the side of the counter to type out a reply.

Me: I'm fine. We ran into RK. Not good.

My teeth sink into my bottom lip, worrying the tender flesh, and I immediately regret mentioning that I saw Ridge to Kelly. She'll want more details and I'm not ready to talk about it. My phone pings with another text.

Kelly: Honey, I'm here if you want to talk. Love you.

Her response surprises me, yet it really shouldn't. She knows how mixed-up I am right now, with no answers to anything, and she isn't pushing. Though the time will come when she'll want me to spill.

I text out thanks and no sooner hit send when she adds another text, making me laugh and cringe at the same time.

Kelly: Oh and I've only broken one glass! Oz isn't too mad.

My chuckles cause several sets of eyes to look my way. *Oh shit.* I'm surrounded by half of the Kincaide clan.

At a large round table across the store, the twins, Jett and Scarlett, as well as the two youngest, Laken and Jasper, sit with their ice creams. None of them are talking.

Lucky me, I have their attention.

It's like I'm back in high school, though Cole Kincaide's missing from this dreadful reunion. Two years my junior, and while I wouldn't say we were friends in high school or otherwise, Cole's all right.

He comes into Oz's every now and then, and through the years has never been mean or arrogant. That's a lot more than I can say about some of them staring at me right now.

Jett's unrelenting stare burns my skin, and sadly, I'm all too familiar with that look. We're the same age and were stuck in the same grade all through school.

His sharp blue eyes roam my body from head to toe in a not-so-subtle and definitely cocky way like it's his God-given right to get his fill. Suddenly, my simple black jeans and T-shirt feel downright scandalous, but I refuse to give a damn.

His twin, Scarlett, and maybe the meaner of the two,

throws me an icy stare before resuming her conversation, and I let out a sigh, grateful for her spiteful silence rather than the nasty insults she'd flung in high school.

Next is Laken, the prettiest cowgirl in all the land—*barf*—and one of the most sought after girls in town. She's talked to me before and was nice enough, but only when we were alone. If she's with her horde of followers, I might as well be invisible.

And then there's Jasper. He's the only one still staring at me with a soft, almost welcoming smile. Funnily enough, as the youngest of the bunch, he has never had any reason to talk to me yet he's one of the nicer ones. And now that he's legal, I've seen him at the club once or twice with his friends.

I sidle up to the counter and place my order, stealing furtive glances at the bunch. Every once in a while, one of them will do the same. Despite it being just the five of us in here, I sit at a small table close to the door.

Scarlett rambles on about some upcoming party or community gathering, the high whine of her voice grating on my nerves. Laken offers the obligatory nods and smiles, while both men bear similar looks, as if they'd rather poke their eyes out with a fork than continue the conversation.

The cold, silky ice cream coats my throat and does its job to fill me up. While eating, I wonder what the likes of the twins, Laken, or Jasper will do when they learn Ridge is going to be a father? And better yet, that I'm the one carrying his baby.

Will my child be ostracized and ridiculed like I was? No mother wants that, or I should say, no loving, responsible mother wants that for their child.

Maybe it's best to keep the paternity a secret. Things could go very wrong if the Kincaides turn their backs on this little one.

Their fingers are in everything and their influence is far-reaching, and I'm not just talking about cutting the child off financially. That would be the least of my worries as thoughts of Travis and his misfortunes stab at my heart.

My hand protectively falls to my belly, and movement from their table draws my attention. Laken cocks her head to one side and openly stares, eyes boring into my stomach where my hand lies, before flicking up to meet mine.

There's something dark and strange, maybe even perceptive, about her gaze, and dread grips my belly. She can't possibly know. Can she?

At most, it might look like I've put on a few pounds—I have even though I'm throwing up daily—but not like I'm pregnant.

I've got to talk to Ridge and settle things once and for all. While his financial support is sorely needed, at one point I hoped he would openly claim the child. Forget about a relationship with me, I wanted him to be a father to his son or daughter. And when I ran into him earlier, I had the sense he might be feeling the same way. Now, I'm not so sure that's a good idea.

With the last spoonful of minty chocolate goodness melting on my tongue, I tear my gaze from Laken, no longer able to stomach any of them. I need out of here.

Dumping the cup in the trash, I walk out into the blinding sun with my mind set on talking to Ridge. As if a sign, or meant to be—none of which I believe in—the man in question strolls toward me.

My heartbeat thunders in my ears.

He's alone and his expression is grim. He opens his mouth, readying to say something, but I beat him to the punch.

"We need to talk." I scan the area. People are going about their business, and so far, no one's looking our way.

"Yes, we do." He wipes at his damp brow and cautiously takes my elbow. "Let's sit over here, in the shade."

Too weary to protest or pull away, I follow him to the gazebo in the small park several doors down at the end of the sidewalk. We're still in plain sight, but somewhat hidden from the cross streets and prying eyes.

I wonder if that's why he chose this spot—not because of the heat or the shade. Who cares, it's just as well.

"Look, I went about this the wrong way." I turn to face him as we sit side by side. "I told you about the pregnancy because you had a right to know, but we need to set boundaries and also hash out a few things."

"Boundaries?" His lips thin, as if he has a sudden distaste for where I'm going with this chat. "What are you talking about?"

"I'm not sugarcoating this. I do need help financially." My stomach somersaults at the admission. I hate this. Hate asking for help. It feels like a handout even if he's just as responsible as I am for this child. "But if—"

He interjects, nostrils flaring, "Of course."

"Okay. But even if you are helping to support the child, you can't disrupt my life on a whim. Earlier today with my brother—that can't happen again. You have no right, even if I'm carrying your child, to cause a scene because I'm talking to someone."

"Lacy, I overreacted. But consider things from my viewpoint. It looked like you were with another man."

"And? So what if I was? Are we together? Engaged or married? Last I checked, we aren't anything and you have no right to act like that."

He stiffens, pressing his lips together, and I can't tell if it's to keep his anger in check or because he's at a loss for words.

"I don't expect any more from you. I'm not demanding you marry me or even be a part of the baby's life. In fact—"

"No, I want to be a part of my child's life." His words are hard and hurried, cutting me off before I have a chance to suggest we keep the paternity under wraps.

I swallow with difficulty, teeth biting at the inside of my cheek. What I'm about to say might hurt. If I were in his shoes, it would cut me to the quick, but it must be said.

"Ridge, think about this. We might want to keep the fact that you are the father a secret." I lick my lips and his head shakes violently, eyes darkening. "You're engaged and this child is..."

A lump the size of a boulder blooms in my throat, making my next words downright painful. "This child is a bastard. The deck is already stacked against him or her."

"Fuck, no," he grits out, cheeks reddening with rage. "I am the father. My child will know me, and I'll do whatever it takes to ensure my son or daughter has what they need. No one will treat them less than. Do you hear me?"

"Okay." I hold up my hands and soften my voice to quell

the rage rolling off him in waves. "I just thought I'd put that out there."

"Heard and answered. We're not keeping it a secret." He rakes a hand through his thick hair, and his blue eyes drill into me. "Besides, I've already told my mother, and I plan on telling the rest of the family soon."

Instinctively, I tense, and my chest constricts. Sage Kincaide knows. *Dammit.*

Then I glance over his shoulder in the direction of Mel's. The ice cream parlor is out of view from where we are, and I have no clue if his brothers and sisters are still there, but my worst fears seem to spring to life.

Ridge may think simply stating he's the father is enough, but I know better. His mother knows about the baby.

Once more, I rub protectively at my stomach. Sage Kincaide will be out for blood, and I'm not so sure if even the heir apparent can stop her.

7

———

RIDGE

*M*ama's icy glare competes with the air conditioner to cool the room. It's the same chilling look she wore all through our lunch with Chastity, almost two weeks ago. A look she's been wearing ever since.

It's strange to have it directed at me.

I don't know what's pissed her off more, me ruining her plans and sullying her reputation by getting someone pregnant out of wedlock or the idea that once she's a grandmother, townsfolk might think of her as old.

Maybe both.

One thing's for sure, with all the pains she goes through to hide her age, she'd be doubly pissed if she knew how much her current scowl draws out the fine lines around the corners of her eyes and mouth.

I just wish she'd say something. *Anything.*

When I dumped the news on her at that lunch, I was

prepared for her rage. Ready for her threats. Open to hear all about her bitter disappointment in me.

But this silence?

It's worse.

Not because I want to hear what a royal screwup she thinks I am, but because the only thing scarier than Sage Kincaide all riled up is when she's silently scheming.

I've never been on this side of her ire before. At least, not to this degree.

Normally, I'd be the one she'd turn to for support. The one who'd help cook up her plan of attack. And I'm all too aware of what she's capable of—more so now that Pa's gone.

"Is this going to take long?" Scarlett complains, sweeping into the room with Jett following closely behind her.

Mama doesn't even spare the twins a glance. Her caustic gaze is still stuck on me, but it doesn't stop her from chastising, all the same. "Why? Do you have someplace better to be? Something more important to attend than your family?"

"Of course not, Mama." Scarlett bows her head and crosses the room to sit on the sofa, at my side.

Jett sits beside her, immediately bending his head to hers, and whispers, "You wouldn't dare."

Oh, but she is a daring one, my sister. Always with a quick tongue and spitfire attitude. Somehow, she manages to stay on Mama's good side. Although truly, I'm not sure whose side she's on, other than Jett's. The two of them are inseparable, and I often wonder if they don't have their own secret agenda in play.

My other siblings arrive in one large pack. Laken, Jasper, and Cole tumble in like the young herd of wildlings they are, all loudly talking and not paying the rest of us any mind. Brooks and his new bride, Addie, are behind them, still looking as stupidly in love as they did on their wedding day. Trey brings up the rear, creeping in like a goddamn spy and taking his usual spot at Mama's side.

The only one missing is Clay, but I didn't expect to see him here, since he's on tour promoting his latest chart-topping country album. Hell, he didn't even have the decency to show up for Pa's funeral or the reading of the will. Fame is more important to him, I guess.

But at least he's got the balls to follow his heart.

"Brooks, I thought you two would finally be on your honeymoon. I'm surprised to see you here," Mama croons.

Only a couple of months ago, she was at his throat, fighting to keep him from taking the head seat of Canyon Spring. Now that he's backed off and is building a life for himself—away from our family empire—she's like a fly on shit and happily his biggest supporter.

"We're postponing it until Greener Prospects is up and running full tilt," Addie answers, referencing their new business venture and wrapping her arms around my brother's waist in a way that seems almost protective.

"And we had those few days up at the cabin. That was a pretty nice little getaway." Brooks beams at his fresh-faced wife, returning her embrace before bending to kiss her forehead like a fool.

Yeah, their lovey-dovey act still makes me a little nauseous.

"Well, I'm glad you're here," Mama says, throwing her

daggered gaze back in my direction. "Glad at least one of you is acting responsibly."

I tamp down the urge to roll my eyes. I'm not a petulant child, and there's no point in poking the bull.

"What's this all about anyway?" Brooks asks.

Mama's lips twitch with a callous smirk. "Same thing it's always about. The future of Canyon Spring Ranch."

A hard knot forms in my stomach, and I ball my hands to white-knuckled fists. Only, I can't keep them from shaking, so I cross my arms over my chest instead.

The urge to lash out is fierce.

But I won't be provoked into self-destruction.

That's exactly what she's looking for, and as much as her veiled threat pisses me off, it can't hurt me. Not really. I've worked too damn hard and given up too fucking much to let her continue pushing me around, grieving or not.

Besides, I'm well-versed in the art of manipulation and can talk my way out of any situation. Mama should know; she taught me herself.

"I have some news I wanted to share with y'all." My voice is calm and measured as I stand, despite the tension trying to rip apart my body. And mind.

Their eyes are all glued to me now.

No pressure.

"Mama's right, this is about the future. Not just the future of the ranch, but the future of this family." *This messed-up, selfish fucking family.*

I pause, not only for dramatic effect but to try and wrangle my wildly pumping heart back under control.

Unfolding my arms, I land my hands on my hips and widen my stance, making myself look as large and imposing as possible.

With a deep breath, I announce, "I'm going to be a father."

Gasps, followed by a few low murmurs and Mama's heavy sigh, greet the news.

"When?" Trey asks, his amber eyes sharply focused and perceptive.

Mama's head tilts in his direction and her mouth stretches to an eerie smile. "Yes, Ridge, do tell us when."

The knot in my stomach pulls painfully tighter. "I'm not sure, exactly." My mind cartwheels as I do the mental math. "In about six months?"

Shit, how do I not already know this? How am I so unprepared?

"Time to go dress shopping," Scarlett says with a giddy clap of her hands.

I swing my gaze to meet hers. "What for?"

"Well, I can't wear the same thing to your wedding that I wore to Brooks's. I assume with this news you'll be hoofing it to the altar ASAP."

I stare at her, incredulous. Her first response to my impending fatherhood is to think about her damn wardrobe?

"There's not going to be a wedding," I force out from between gritted teeth.

"What?" Mama's tone turns downright glacial. "What do you mean, no wedding? What about Chastity? You can't just turn your back on her; we have an agreement in place."

"Wait," Laken drawls. Her brow furrows dramatically as she puts pieces of the puzzle together, and I fear I might've pushed the moral boundaries for my innocent little sister. "Chastity isn't the one who's pregnant?"

"No." My neck stiffens and nostrils flare as I turn to Mama. "I've put a lot of thought into this, which is why I've waited so long to tell everyone. And I've decided I don't give a damn about any deal with her or her family. It's not even a good one—not for us, anyway."

"Ridge." Mama looks like a rabid animal, with her teeth bared in an aggressive snarl. "The terms of your father's will—"

"I don't give a damn about that either," I say, cutting her off. "If I'm going to be head of this ranch, then I say his last wishes were exactly that, Mama. *Wishes.*"

Blood pumps hard through my veins as I meet her feral stare with my own. "What we're talking about now are facts. And the fact is that I will not abandon my child or its mother. You know Chastity won't have any part of me once she hears that."

"Besides," I continue, dropping my voice to ensure she's listening close. "Do you really think Pa would want a Kincaide baby to be raised without the influence of this family? Without its father?"

Her eyes grow wide, and she sits back in her seat, visibly shaken. She nods absently but doesn't utter a word, her mouth pinched into a hard line.

"So, if Chastity isn't the mother, then who is?" Laken asks, her voice as uncertain as the look on her beautiful young face.

Slowly, I scan the room, my measured gaze meeting each of those around me, silently daring someone to argue, before coming back to Mama's hollow stare.

With my head held high, I tell them, "Lacy Hallman."

No one has much to say after that.

Scarlett asks a few more questions—all of them tied to shopping somehow—and Cole dares to wonder aloud if Chastity might be open to dating, but without Mama leading the conversation, it's soon over.

She stands, brushing invisible wrinkles from her clothes, and without another word, leaves the room.

My siblings all quickly follow.

"Ridge," Addie calls, her voice soft but steady.

I turn to the doorway where she lingers with Brooks, who seems amiable. They're the only two left in the room.

"Congratulations," she says with a pretty smile. "To Lacy too."

"Thanks," I mumble, unsure what else to say.

These two should hate me after everything I helped Mama put them through. Yet, of all my family, they're the only ones that seem to give a damn.

But that's just fine by me.

If Pa taught me anything about running this place, it's that I don't need my family's love to do it. All I need is for them to understand that I'm the one in charge.

The fan overhead continues its soft rotation, just like the earth under my feet.

I told them. What could've been a dirty little secret is now out in the open, and nothing fell apart. Even Mama seemed resigned to the idea by the end. Maybe this thing isn't as big or scary as I first thought.

Or maybe this is just the calm before the storm.

With Lacy, a squall seems inevitable. But some weird part of me looks forward to it. To her wildness. Her intensity.

Fuck. I need to get the hell out of this house. Away from the stifling conditioned air and beige walls. Away from my overbearing family and the expectations that come along with them. Somewhere private, where I can talk to my woman.

Because whether Lacy knows it yet or not, she is mine. At least, I'm aiming to make her mine—sooner than fucking later, I hope.

I stalk outside and hop in my truck. My foot is heavy on the accelerator as I tear away from the house, but I don't go far.

Only a few miles away, I pull off the road and bump along a dusty old path until I reach the thick copse of trees and the open, somewhat hidden valley beyond it.

I love this spot. My brother Brooks thinks it's his little secret, but it isn't—I followed him here one night and have been sneaking off to it on my own ever since.

With the windows down, I shut off the engine of my truck, but don't bother getting out. This place is private, yet something about the added security of the steel cage around me gives me the courage to do what comes next.

I fish my phone from my pocket and dial Lacy's number. It's amazing the information I can round up, all because my last name's Kincaide.

"Hello?"

The minute I hear her voice, the heavy ball of tension in my gut begins to slowly unravel.

"Hey, Lace. Am I catching you at a bad time?"

There's hesitation on the other end of the line, and for a moment I wonder if the call's dropped, until finally she replies, "Sort of. I was just about to hop in the shower."

Images of her naked with rivulets of water running over her smooth skin, down the valley between her full breasts and soaking her thick mane of hair invade my senses. Instantly, I'm hard—a condition that seems to be permanently evoked by thoughts of her.

"Ridge?" she calls. "Is everything all right?"

"Yeah. Yeah, everything's fine." I clear my throat, hit by a sudden bout of nerves. "I just wanted you to know that I told them. I told my family about the baby."

"You did?" Her voice is soft, unsure. "How did that go?"

"Better than expected. They're all really happy for us."

"They are?"

Fuck, I can't lie—at least, not to her. I don't know why that is, and maybe it should have me panicked, but with Lacy, all I ever feel is calm. Still, those emotions are a lot to unpack, and I've got more than enough on my plate to deal with for now.

"Well, no one threw a tantrum or had to be punched in the face," I say, walking a fine line between truth and lie. "So at least they're not completely unhappy. And Brooks and Addie said to tell you congratulations."

"Okay, well, that's nice." Skepticism laces her words. It's

not quite a brush-off, but she's clearly not invested in the outcome of this conversation. Not like me. "Listen, I should go..."

"Lacy," I call, an urgent pull of desire straining my voice, "when can I see you? I really think we should talk face-to-face. Alone."

"It hasn't been that long since we last talked, and I think we could use some space. You need time to sort things out, and I'm not so sure about being alone with you right now. After everything that went down on Main Street..."

"Again, I'm sorry about that. I promise, I would never hurt you. I hope you know I've never laid a hand on a woman, and I never would. At least, not an unwanted one."

"Oh, I know." Her voice comes out sounding strangled. Is that a bit of lust tinting her tone? "Listen, I really do need to go...the water's running."

"Okay, Lace. Enjoy that shower, and I'll talk to you soon." Until I do, I'll be thinking about her.

As much as I'd like to say it, I keep that truth to myself. She's not ready to hear it.

Frustrated and turned on, I toss my phone on the truck console. The buildup of tension has me nearly crawling out of my skin.

God, she turns me on. Every little thing about her.

Not just my X-rated mental image of her, but the tone of her voice, and even the scrappy reactions she gives me. She's so damn genuine, tenacious, curvy and... *fuck.*

I can't take any more of this torture. After a quick look around to ensure I'm alone, I pop open my fly and ease out my aching cock.

Already rock hard, it won't take much to get myself off. Still, my fist is a poor replacement for the real thing—Lacy's tight, slick heat.

The sensation of sliding deep inside her is still a vivid memory, and I hold on to that feeling—that inexplicable fucking euphoria—as I stroke myself to completion.

8

LACY

I'd kill to sleep. I lazily amble up the steps to the second-floor apartments, running on empty and dreaming of my bed.

Like usual, it's quiet at two in the morning, most people fast asleep. Every part of my body aches, which isn't new for being on my feet for the better part of ten hours, but I'm feeling extra raw. The nausea made an appearance tonight, which sucked, even if it didn't stay long.

And I've heard pregnant women are tired, like all the time. It's something about all the body is doing, constantly working to make a little human, and yet it also feels like torture. The body's way of preparing you for the constant state of sleep deprivation once the baby is born.

Who knows why exhaustion dominates your life for nine months, or is it twenty years? Either way, I've never known fatigue like this before and I'm only past the first trimester.

Tonight, the club was crazy, and all I wanted to do was

curl up in a ball under the bar. Never mind the sticky shit on the floor; I didn't care. All I wanted was sleep.

Still do. I could sleep for the rest of my life.

The men were plentiful and rowdy, and tonight was go, go, go. So much so, I had to skip my breaks because we were constantly backed up on the drink orders. And while the night's behind me, thank goodness, the tips were amazing. I shouldn't complain.

My hair sticks to the nape of my neck, damp and matted. A shower and bed... I am steps away from heaven.

Once on the second floor of the small, two-story, eight-unit building, I stop to catch my breath and wish, like I do every time, that there was an elevator. That's when I freeze. A dark figure looms in front of my apartment door.

"Lacy Hallman," the male shadow, voice deep and rough, calls.

Fear causes mayhem in my already sensitive stomach, and I squeeze the keys in my hand while the other tightens its grip on the railing. I could run. But I wouldn't get too far. I'm exhausted, and I can't risk it, not with the baby.

He's tall, broad-shouldered, imposing with a cowboy hat on but tipped down. Most likely deliberate because I can't see his face. Slight movement behind him is another kick to the chest. He isn't alone. There's someone else with him, but I can't make out who.

It doesn't help that the overhead hallway lights are out. They don't work and haven't for weeks now. I've been after the super, Oz's deadbeat nephew who's supposed to maintain the building in exchange for free rent, to replace the lights.

"Lacy," the man repeats, nearing me. "We just want to talk."

"Not another step. Stay right where you are." I inch back toward the stairs. "Who the hell are you?"

He pulls something from the pocket of his pants, and I prepare to run or scream "fire" or something when he flicks on a flashlight of what looks to be his phone. The bright beam shines in my direction, nearly blinding me.

"Get that thing out of my face," I holler, now more mad than scared.

He casts the white light onto his face and that of the person who is now standing beside him.

Holy shit. Trey and Sage Kincaide.

This night. I wanted it to end before it began and figured it couldn't get any worse. I was wrong. So very wrong.

The beam dips to the floor and stays there. Both of them stare expectantly at me.

"What do you want to talk about that couldn't keep until daylight?" I don't want to talk to either of them—not now, not ever—but I suppose I shouldn't be surprised to see them. "You showing up like this, standing in the dark outside a woman's home, that's just wrong. Were you looking to scare me half to death?"

I don't hide my irritation. I've never been one to hold my tongue and I'm not going to start now. Especially not for the likes of the Kincaides. Tired and grumpy, these people are keeping me from my bed, and I'm more than sure that nothing good will come from this.

"Apologies. You're a hard woman to get alone. Went to Oz's, hoping to catch you on a break, but you were always behind the bar." Trey places his hands on his hips, dipping his head in somewhat of a humble gesture.

My heart speeds up at his words. He was at the club tonight? Was Sage there too? Why didn't I see them? Why would they go there? A cold chill skates up my spine, only confirming the dread mounting within me.

"Let's go inside." Sage slides out from behind Trey, mirroring him with her hands on her hips.

Are they trying to intimidate me? I can't make out her features because of the darkness, but I can imagine her eyes narrowing into thin blade-like slits. She must be shooting daggers at me. It's all there in her voice.

I swallow with difficulty, my throat suddenly parched, and the urge to vomit rears its ugly head again.

Not in my home. I don't want these two in my house. This is my safe place, away from the likes of these vultures. Besides, it's small and dingy. I'm not embarrassed of what is mine, though they'll think it's a hellhole.

"Talk here." My arms cross my chest, and I will the little food in my stomach to stay put.

Trey sighs, Sage scoffs, and this cues my eye roll. For the first time since setting eyes on them, I'm grateful for the night and shadows. I can't see her face.

"For God's sakes, open the door. This is ridiculous. It's bad enough we're loitering in a hallway in the middle of the night." Aggravation blankets her voice. "Let us in so we can talk. The sooner we do, the sooner we're gone."

They aren't going anywhere until they get their way. This is clear to see and so typical of the Kincaides. Without another word, I unlock the door, step into my cool apartment, and flick on a light.

Once I'm only a few feet inside, I spin on my heel to face them and hold up my hands. "Stop. This is as far as you're going."

She releases a long drawn-out sigh and presses her lips together but doesn't try to change my mind.

Surprisingly, neither one presses to come in any farther, both gazes darting around the room. My back's to my home but I know what they see. Clothes strewn all over the small living room.

They're clean. I did laundry earlier today before work but ran out of time to fold and put them away. None of that matters. All they see is trash and Sage proves that's so when her upper lip curls in disgust.

"Stay right here. I need to get some water." I lick my dry lips and hurry to the kitchen.

Normally, I'd offer my guests a drink, but these two weren't invited and I'm making sure they know it. I haven't forgotten my manners. Instead I'm choosing not to be hospitable.

My place is small enough that they aren't out of my sight while I down two glasses before my thirst is somewhat quenched. Leaving the glass on the counter, I wipe my mouth with the back of my hand and join them at the entrance.

Arching a brow in question, I urge them to get to the purpose of their visit. I'm readying for their assault. There's no mistaking that's what this is.

"I'll keep this short seeing as it's an ungodly hour and I've got better things to do." Sage is off to a fabulous start, and I huff, causing her to pause at my contempt. "Get rid of the baby or leave town. Those are your choices."

"Excuse me?" I heard her just fine, and a small part of me isn't shocked by the demand, but the nerve of this woman.

"I'll pay for an abortion and give you enough money to start over somewhere else."

"No."

"Then, I'll give you enough money to leave town now. You can start over someplace else and have the baby there. But you're to never return to Prospect or contact Ridge. Ever again."

My exhaustion takes a back seat to my outrage. "What part of no don't you get?"

"You're not understanding. You're lucky I'm even giving you a choice." Anger blazes from her stony gaze. "I will not have your illegitimate child running around this town, sullying the Kincaide name, and giving the gossips something to chew on for years to come."

The woman waggles her finger at me, stepping closer as if I'm hard of hearing. My blood boils. The conversation with Ridge, his call to tell me he told his family about the baby, flashes in my mind.

He sounded hopeful whereas despair swamps me. Is he really naïve enough to believe all would be fine?

Ridge doesn't strike me as stupid or gullible. He must have expected this at the very least. Or maybe he's in on this shakedown. Maybe he knows his mama's here, making demands, and this way he doesn't have to be the bad guy.

Nah, that doesn't feel right.

Ridge isn't a bullshitter.

If he wanted nothing to do with this baby—with me— he'd have told me without any remorse.

"I will not have you destroying Ridge's life or the family business." Her voice cuts through my thoughts and her rant yanks me back to the present.

"You done?" I step around them, curling my hand on the doorknob. "Let me make myself clear. I can't be bought. This is my life, and as far as this baby is concerned, only two people get to have a say about its future. And that's Ridge and me. So get out."

I fling the door open and glare, willing them to try me. Trey and Sage exchange a glance. His is more one of retreat but hers...

She's the general and never willing to give up a fight. "Name your price."

I scoff and pause for a second, wanting to say something outlandish like a million dollars, but don't. I'm afraid she might say yes. Not that I'd take the money—as tempting as it would be. I just don't want to know how far she's willing to go to get her way.

"I'm not for sale."

"We'll see about that. Everyone's for sale for the right price." She storms out of my apartment, and instantly, I can breathe easier.

Trey stares, without any indication that he plans to follow his mother any time soon.

I narrow my gaze on him. "Get out of my home."

"She means business." His tone is softer, as is his expression, than when his mother was in the room.

"I feel like you're deaf or something." I still don't like or trust him, but I'm not as on edge with only him in my place. "I don't want your money."

"I'm overstepping here." He sticks his head out into the hallway as if checking to make sure Sage is gone.

"You think?" If I had the strength, I'd kick him out and slam the door in his face.

"Don't be the hero or martyr. If you want this baby, take the money and leave. That's the smart option. Name your price. She'll pay it." As if he's already said too much, he mashes his lips together and stares hard at me.

"My answer hasn't changed. No. Now get out." I clench my jaw and ball my fists at my sides.

I'm done being civil and I'm now on the verge of tears.

Damn hormones. I will not let him see me cry. Fuck him and his mother.

He sighs, shaking his head like he's gravely disappointed in me. *Poor Lacy, dumber than dirt.*

"I don't need to tell you this, but just in case you're thinking of doing this on your own. Don't." He pauses and runs his thumb across his lower lip like he's weighing his next words. "Tell Ridge about this. He'll be pissed and it'll cause problems with Sage, but he'd want to know. And"—again, he glances outside and then back to me—"if you're planning on sticking around, you've got a long road ahead of you. Telling Sage to fuck off isn't the end. It's only the beginning. You've declared war, a battle you can't imagine, and you'll need Ridge at your side."

9

——————

RIDGE

y head hurts as I reshuffle the same stack of papers I've been working on all morning. Despite my need to stay occupied and get some real work done, I can't concentrate for shit.

My mind has been running circles since Lacy dropped the news about the baby. Ever since my baser instincts took over and I declared my intentions to my entire family.

Well, not all of my intentions. Sure as hell not going to tell them how I plan to win her over and make her mine. Or how my preferred way to do that is by getting her naked again, then making her beg for more.

Fuck me.

When did I become so infatuated? So goddamn possessive?

And why the hell do I like it so much?

There's a hard knock on my office door, and the pain at my temple flares. I'm not in the mood for any more of my family's nosiness, and not in the right headspace to deal with anything important pertaining to the ranch.

But I can't ignore duty forever. "Come in."

The door bursts open, revealing the woman I've been obsessing over, and the look on her face tells me I'm in for a world of hurt.

Damn, she's gorgeous.

She stomps forward, closing the door firmly behind her, and crosses her arms under her ample breasts, making my dick perk up and take notice.

"I am not for sale."

Her words crash over me like a dousing of cold water. "Pardon?"

"You heard me. I cannot be bought or sold like some cow at market. I don't want to leave town to suit someone else's agenda, and I will *not* have an abortion."

"Fucking right you won't. That's my child you're carrying, and I already told you I'm taking care of what's mine. Where's this all coming from, Lace?"

Her eyes turn watery, and on a heavy sigh she drops her arms like the fight's been suddenly drained from her. She looks like she's ready to collapse, and a jolt of panic surges through me.

I stand, knocking back my chair, and rush to her side, ready to catch her if she falls. "You okay? Why don't you sit and tell me what's going on."

Her nod is almost imperceptible, and she refuses to look me in the eye, but she lets me lead her to the nearby chair and takes a seat.

I kneel in front of her, taking one of her hands in mine,

hoping for her attention. Her lips form a tight line, and her gaze bounces around the room, like she'd rather be anywhere but here.

With a growl, I grasp her chin, forcing her to look at me. "Tell me, Lace. Now."

She lets out a strangled sort of sound—her eyes now brimming with something that looks a helluva lot like lust, along with the tears.

But I ignore the building pressure behind my zipper.

"Your mother..." Her words are barely a whisper, but they ring loud and clear.

Truthfully, she doesn't need to say another word for me to understand, but I want to hear it anyway. I need to know the details of what duplicitous shit Mama's up to now.

"She offered me money." Her chin wobbles despite her obvious effort not to cry. "Told me I could either get rid of the baby or get out of town. She didn't care which, but either way, it was clear she wants me gone."

Rage so potent it hurts claws its way up my spine. "Fucking bitch."

"Excuse me?" Lacy pulls back like I've slapped her, yanking her hand out of mine.

"Not you." Both outraged and insulted, I push my hand through my hair to stop myself from reaching out for her again. As much as I want to comfort her, it's clear touching her right now would be a mistake.

"She's your mother, Ridge. You're telling me you didn't see this coming?"

My gut reaction is to deny it, but didn't I foresee a scenario exactly like this playing out? I knew Mama wouldn't just accept this and move on. I knew her mixed-up sense of family values would never allow me to be anything less than her grandest vision.

Still, it's hard to admit my own flesh and blood would stoop so low, regardless of her reasoning. "She thinks she's protecting me."

Lacy huffs, her lips twisting to a pretty scowl, her body still rigid and withdrawn.

Fuck, how does her hostility turn me on so damn much, even when I'm near to bursting with anger?

"I know. It's a rotten and pathetic excuse. But it's the only one I've got."

"Do you really think you should be making excuses for her?"

"No, you're right. And I know giving in to her whims so often is what's allowed her to become as terrible as she is."

A sick feeling takes hold as I think of all the times I've looked the other way. Or worse, gotten my hands dirty and colluded in one of her schemes. I never even second-guessed her, especially not when it helped me get my own way.

Hell, I even backed her in screwing over my own brother, all so I'd get the thing I was always promised...

Control.

I take Lacy's hand again, thankful when she doesn't pull away. "I've always played her games. Always figured it was better to be on her side than fighting her. But not this time."

She squeezes my fingers, and I carry on, empowered by the connection. "I promise you, Lace, I'll talk to her. Put her in her place. I won't let this stand."

"Ridge..." She leans toward me, with a hint of resignation

in her gaze. "I'm not going to pretend to understand your family or the rules you all play by. And honestly, I don't care what you have to do to make her stop. Just...please make her stop."

Her brow furrows and her gaze bores into mine. "And leave me alone to raise this baby the best I can."

It takes every ounce of willpower I possess not to grab her and kiss the hell out of her until she caves to my desires. Instead, I run my free hand up the side of her leg, only stopping when I reach her waist.

She sucks in an audible breath when I shift my hand, ever so slightly, and stroke my thumb over her stomach.

"You're not doing this alone," I vow.

"But I—"

"No." I can't handle the thought of her struggling for another minute on her own. "No fucking way. I don't know how many times I need to say it, or what I need to do to show you how serious I am. You are *not* doing this alone."

"Okay."

It's only one word, but it feels like I just scaled a mountain. One tiny word, and my future is suddenly within reach.

My real future. One I make for myself, instead of one forced on me by familial obligation. A chance to be not only be head of Canyon Spring, but to have someone at my side who I want there. A chance to be happy.

"Okay?" I test it out. How far can this one word go?

"I guess it's only fair to give you a chance. For the baby's sake." Her plump bottom lip disappears between her teeth, and my cock stands at attention.

She pins me with her arresting dark eyes. "But I don't do

second chances. And it's just for the baby. You and me... We're never going to be together."

I can't help my cocky grin.

And from her reaction, I'd say that's probably a good thing.

She leans closer still, her expression severe and her breath coming in short, shallow bursts. "I'm serious."

"I know you are, and it looks fucking good on you. Makes me want to kiss that smart, pretty mouth of yours."

"Ridge," she groans.

That's it. That one sinful sound is all it takes for my composure to snap. What little of it I had left.

I push up into her space and capture her mouth with mine.

In an instant, she's opening for me—not just her luscious lips, but her thighs part as well, allowing me to wedge myself between them.

She's hot, persistent, and possibly the best thing that's ever happened to me.

My fingers tangle in her long, dark hair, and stroke over the graceful column of her neck. She returns the sentiment, raking her nails over my scalp and shoulders.

"Fuck, Lace," I growl into her mouth. "I want you."

She freezes, her body rigid, and despite wanting nothing more than to finish what we've started, I pause.

She tears her mouth from mine, covering it momentarily with her delicate hand, like she can still feel me there.

"I'm sorry." She backs farther away. "This was a mistake."

Not trusting myself—or more like, my body—I stand and

stalk the length of the room, taking in some much-needed air, away from her intoxicating scent.

When I turn back toward her, she's standing too. "I should go."

"Please, don't." It sounds like I'm begging, something I've never fucking done nor ever expected to do. "Let's talk... nothing more. Let's figure this out."

"Figure what out, exactly? You said you'll deal with your mother, and I said I'd give you a chance to be in your child's life. There's nothing more to discuss."

"Really? Don't you think—"

I'm interrupted by a short tap on the door, right before it swings open.

Chastity. Fuck, I almost forgot about her. We haven't spoken since our lunch with Mama—since the day I decided to upend my entire life—and it was easy to put her out of my mind when she never took up much space there to begin with, but I'm the one who left the message, inviting her here today.

"Oh, pardon me," she says, her hand flying to her chest and eyes going wide in fake surprise. "I didn't realize you had any business meetings today. It wasn't on your schedule."

"It's fine." Lacy turns to face the intruder, head held high and spine ramrod straight. "I was just leaving."

"Lacy, wait. We're not done here."

Looking over her shoulder, she pierces me with dark eyes, now brimming with new tears. "Yes. We are."

Without a second glance, she walks away, leaving me alone with Chastity, whose lips are pinched and glare is stone cold.

"Who was that?" Her demanding tone grates on my last nerve. This woman has acted like she's had ownership over me from day one. Like it's her right to order me around.

News flash, sweetheart—not anymore. "She's none of your damn business."

"Some strange *woman* is in your office without an appointment, and you think it's not my business?" The indignation she's now wearing doesn't seem fake, although it's hard to tell when the rest of her seems so manufactured. "As your fiancée, I think I have a right."

"The wedding's off." No point sugarcoating it. "The entire deal is done. I don't want to marry you."

"Who is she?"

"Christ, Chastity. Did you hear me?"

"Yes, I heard you. I just want to know who she is...who's so much better than me that you'd break the agreement?"

I hang my head with a sigh. "Aren't you sick of playing these ludicrous games? Getting married because our families made a deal? Is that really how you want to live your life?"

Her shoulders droop, and for the first time since I met her, she looks downright human.

So much so, I almost feel sorry for her. "I'm not trying to be an asshole here. I just think we both deserve to be with someone we care about. Someone we love."

My gut tightens, the word *love* leaving me breathless.

Hell, am I in love with Lacy? I don't know if I even believe in it, let alone am capable of it. Plus, I hardly know her.

But her supple curves, spitfire attitude, and steadfast determination sure do make me feel *something*. Add in the way she's already fiercely protecting her child...*our* child.

Fuck, I'm a goddamn goner.

"Hey, Ridge." Mack walks through the open door. "Oh, hey Chastity."

She ignores the burly redhead blocking her exit, and her focus lasers in on me. "I get it. You think you're better than I am."

This woman really doesn't know when to quit. "No," I say honestly, "but I do think marrying you would be a mistake. Besides, you don't really want me."

"How on earth would you know what I want? You make all these assumptions, but not once ever tried to get to know me."

"Well, I know you've got no interest in being a stepmom. And that *woman* who just left here? She's carrying my child."

Mack mumbles something unintelligible and backs into the hallway, almost knocking over my sister Laken in the process.

Chastity's mouth opens and closes a few times, and her hands strangle the purse strap slung over her shoulder.

It seems I've shocked her speechless.

"Look..." I turn my palms up to show I'm no threat and take a step toward her.

She snarls. "Fine." And, turning on her heel, storms away, brushing past Mack and Laken as though they're not there.

They both turn to me...well, no...Mack looks at me, but Laken's eyes are glued to my best friend, like some lovesick little dove.

"What the hell do you want?" I snap.

His bushy eyebrows draw together in a frown. "Thought maybe you'd like to have lunch."

"I was just coming to let you know there's extra in the kitchen if you want some," Laken gushes before rushing away with her face bright as a tomato.

"Goddammit, that's the last thing I need."

"Lunch?"

Ah, you innocent fucking fool.

But if Mack's a fool, what the hell does that make me?

10

LACY

Jesus Christ, what did I just do? I kissed Ridge. Not smart. I went over there to tell him about his mother, to get her to back off. Next thing I know, I'm opening my mouth and my legs for him. I know better. That's what got me into this mess in the first place.

Stop it. We were both single, consenting adults at the time, and we had one night of pleasure. There's no sin or shame in that.

My hand protectively rubs the now slight bump of my stomach. I'm still not showing. No one would see any difference to look at me, but I do.

I lick at my swollen lips and amble down the sidewalk, past the shops in town. Ridge is still taking up space in my head—or more specifically, his soft, firm lips against mine, warm tongue diving into my mouth, and those strong, demanding hands are. The way his fingers dug into my flesh.

Hard and possessive. My panties are wet just thinking about it.

He felt so good. Too good. I wanted to forget all the bull-shit and melt into him. Let him have me. Let me have him.

Dammit.

My hands drive into my unruly hair, and I curl my fingers into the thick strands and pull. The slight sting is the distrac-tion I'm looking for.

My mind can't be filled with silly, futile thoughts of Ridge Kincaide. I'm not a young girl with a senseless crush. We can't be together. It would never work.

Still, I've never felt need that strong in my entire life. The need for a man. If I didn't know better, I'd say I was falling.

A prickly rush of dread sprints up my spine and my steps falter.

"Argh. Stop this." I stomp my foot like a petulant child not getting their way, and a young boy and his mama give me a wide berth as they pass, as though my sulking is contagious.

For crying out loud, these hormones have my mind and body all over the place. Here I am acting out in the middle of town and jumping to foolish conclusions like I might be in love with Ridge.

Love? Where the hell did that come from?

Good God, I don't love Ridge Kincaide.

I don't even believe in true love and all that crap.

Love's a useless, fairy-tale emotion, and it's never helped me or Travis. When we were scared, alone, and starving, love never kept us warm, comforted us, and filled our bellies. Uh-uh, never.

Sure, I'll love my baby. I already do, and a child needs love. But more importantly, they need shelter, food, and a stable home. I'll do my best to provide all of that for my child, but a little help would be nice.

And as much as I hate taking handouts or worse, feeling like I owe somebody, I *owe* it to my child to try and make things work with Ridge in a way that we're civil to one another and our baby gets the best of both of us.

What matters is my baby has a father. No. Not just a father. I have one of those and look what little good that did me. No, this baby needs a good man, a caring and kind father, one that will always be there for their child.

Despite how different our worlds are, or that his family was sent straight from hell—okay, maybe not all of them, but most—Ridge is a good man. He would be a good father.

As much as I hate to admit it, and if Travis were here he'd tell me to shut up, if this baby can have both its parents and I have the power to make it so, then what I have to do is inevitable. My feelings, hurt or otherwise, don't matter.

The whine of my name snaps me out of my wanderings, and I blink at the blonde woman standing in front of me.

"Lacy Hallman. That's you, right?" The way she says my name, as if it hurts to acknowledge me, is as harsh and glaring as the sun.

It's Chastity what's-her-face. Ridge's fiancée.

When she showed up in his office, for one brief moment I worried she'd seen us kissing. Then I didn't give a fuck. And now, either way, it's clear she has a purpose. Did she seek me out? Follow me from Ridge's office?

Whether this run-in is by design or coincidence, it's clear I'm not going to like what she has to say.

"Lacy." She snaps her coral-painted fingertips a mere inch from my face. "You in there?"

Slowly I step back from her, square my shoulders, and narrow my gaze into what I hope looks like the sharp, unforgiving edge of a knife's blade. "What do you want, Chastity?"

"Oh, so you do know who I am?" She brushes a nonexistent stray hair from her face.

Every strand on her head is firmly slicked back with the ends of her bob curled up in a flip. She's pretty in a "I just sucked on a lemon" sort of way, and if I didn't know him, I could almost understand what Ridge sees in her. *Almost.*

She glowers at me expectantly and I remain mute. Her question isn't worth a response.

Impatient, her nostrils flare and she straightens her shoulders on a *humph.* "If you know who I am, which you clearly do"—her lips pucker tightly—"then why are you sniffing around my husband?"

My smirk spreads a mile wide at her blatant misgiving. "Husband? I'm guessing you mean Ridge?"

"Of course I mean Ridge. There's no one else I'd be talking about."

An irksome flush creeps from her neck into her face, and this time, I don a full-on smile. If she could see how easily she'd pass for a cock's comb—the crown-like, fleshy crest found on the top of a rooster's head—I'm pretty sure she'd faint right here on the spot.

"Well then, did I miss something? Did you two have a wedding ceremony because last I heard, y'all were engaged?"

I further exaggerate my sarcasm on the final word just so she knows that I know she's full of shit.

The reddening of her face deepens. "Listen here. You stay away from him, you whore."

She strides past me, nose in the air, and as much as I want to slap her or lob a few nasty words of my own at her, I can't be bothered. I couldn't care less what she thinks of me, but it does make me wonder if she knows that Ridge and I have slept together. And if so, does this mean she knows about the baby?

What's left of the hour before my shift rushes by as I finish my errands and make it behind the bar with a minute to spare. Any thoughts of Ridge, Sage, or even that pesky fly, Chastity, have no room in my head.

Oz's is much like every other night. Time stops for no one. The men keep coming in, drinking, and dropping cash. And as exhausted and achy as I feel, I hardly have time to breathe let alone take a break.

I moan in relief when closing time arrives and the bar is clear of customers. Jem, our stage guy and all around handyperson, flips on most of the lights, and one of the girls hollers, "Hallelujah. Quitting time." A few laugh, offering similar sentiments.

Throughout my shift, I usually try to keep the bar tidy to lessen the time needed for cleanup at the end of the night. I'm almost ready to leave when a dark shadow eclipses me.

I stuff tonight's cash from the register into an envelope before looking up. Ridge stands on the other side of the bar, giving me a devilish, lopsided grin.

Broad shoulders, wide solid chest, and the corded

muscles in his arms on display, I don't know where to look and yet, I can't help but drink him in. Every single muscle in his body is precisely defined. I should know.

My palms burn and the tips of my fingers tingle. I've had my hands on every square inch of him.

Screw my life. I slam my eyes closed to shut out the vision of him and hopefully kill the churning desire growing within me.

When I open them again, I busy myself with grabbing a cloth to wipe down the bar. "How'd you get in here? We're closed."

I'm already rankled before he even opens his mouth, not needing his confirmation of how he smooth talked his way past Gentry, or more likely, threw him some cash to look the other way. The bouncer has two kids from two different women, lots of mouths to feed. Money gets you anything, especially in a place like this.

"I have my ways." He slides onto a bar stool, and the heat of his gaze warms me from head to toe. "I wanted to take you home."

My head snaps up to look at him. "I'm getting a ride with Kelly. I'm fine."

"Fucking right you are—finest damn thing I've ever seen." His smoldering blue eyes peruse my chest, hair, eyes, and eventually land on my lips, lingering there. "But I want to take you home. I want us to finish our conversation from earlier."

"Nothing else to say." I spin away from the bar, but he's quick.

Long, calloused fingers curl around my wrist, firm but

gentle, keeping me in place. "Lace, come on, we aren't done. We're only getting started."

He pushes from the stool and leans his broad frame over the bar. His nose lingers only a breath from mine, and his dark gaze dips once more to my lips. They are slightly parted, begging for air to fill my lungs.

My pulse races and I shift anxiously, tempted to pull away but thinking better of it. Ridge isn't going to let me go, and truth be told, I'm right where I want to be. His hand on me, warm breath skating over my face, eyes devouring me.

Why do I have to want him so? Things would be a heck of a lot easier if this man didn't turn me into a puddle like an ice cube in a heat wave whenever he's near.

"Ridge—" I start, but Kelly pops her head in between us.

"Is everything okay?" Her tiny body is practically on the bar, and her eyes narrow on Ridge.

I stifle a laugh, not sure if it's to break the electric connection with Ridge or because my girl can't do pissed off no matter how hard she tries. Well, except at Travis.

"Kel, we're fine." I drag my gaze to my best friend while gently trying to tug my arm from Ridge's hold.

He isn't budging.

Slowly, she slides her feet back onto the ground, eyeing us skeptically. "Are you sure?"

"We're just talking." He flashes her his pearly whites. "I'm taking Lace home." There's no room for negotiation in his tone, and I want to scream. But I don't.

With his eyes on me, he asks my friend, "Are you okay to get home or do you need a ride?"

I want to call him out. He knows she has her own car

because I just told him so, but his concern seems genuine. I have no doubt if she wanted a ride, he'd do it no problem and even arrange for her car to get to her place.

"I'm fine, thanks." Kel's gaze drifts from Ridge to me. "Lacy?"

Without any words, her look says everything. She wants to make sure I'm all right, and I convey as much, adding in a nod for good measure. "Okay. Good night."

Ridge loosens his grip on my wrist but doesn't let go. "Kelly, do you need me to walk you to your car?"

Fuck him for being chivalrous. Usually, I hate that kind of shit, but for some reason my girly bits are fluttering and warming because he cares about my best friend.

"No, I'm good. Gentry will walk me. Night." She waves at us and saunters to the exit.

I yank on my arm and grit my teeth. "Let go of me."

Ridge swings back to face me. "I called off the engagement."

My heart stutters. "What?"

He releases me and slides back onto the stool. "You heard me. I'm not marrying Chastity. And like I said, you and I have plenty to talk about."

My insides somersault and I'm unable to look at him as I wipe down the bar for the final time. It doesn't need it.

"Why'd you go and do that? Your mama's going to tan your hide." His news has sparked something inside of me.

Electricity sizzles and liquefies my insides. I twirl the cloth into a long, tight funnel and slash it against the wood of the bar. The lightning snap, so like a whip, crackles through the air.

He chuckles at my implication of how his mother will react, but there's a rigidity to his posture that doesn't lessen with the shake of his body. And the tiny lines around his eyes and mouth multiply and deepen as if there's truth to my words.

"Yeah, well, I spoke with her too. Told her in no uncertain terms you were not to be messed with."

"And she listened?"

"I didn't give her much of a choice." The harsh edge of his voice makes me shiver. "She understands my position and won't bother you again."

Despite his conviction, doubt swirls through me. What's the likelihood of Sage Kincaide doing what anyone tells her?

Still, he's trying, and don't I owe it to him—to our child— to at least give him a chance?

"Thank you." I offer a curt nod, hoping like hell he's right and his mother will leave me alone. Even as a needy, foolish part of me hopes he won't.

When we arrive at my apartment, he insists on walking me up and coming in. He shuts the door behind him. "I don't want you working at Oz's anymore."

I pull off my boots and curl my toes into the carpet. "Don't start. How else am I going to live?"

"I'll take care of you." He follows me into the small living room as though he belongs here—belongs with me and in my life.

"Uh-uh. I don't need that. All I need is for you to take care of your child. Be there for this baby." Instinctively, my hand goes to my stomach.

His gaze lands on my belly and he smiles. "Of course, that

goes without saying. But Lace." He softens his tone and takes my hand. "Taking care of you is taking care of the baby. You shouldn't be working there. Just look at you."

I pull my hand from his. "What the hell is that supposed to mean?"

With a heavy sigh, he guides me to sit on the couch. "You're exhausted. Being on your feet all day can't be good."

Before I can protest, he sits next to me and pulls my leg onto his lap, my foot in his hands. His fingers knead and rub at the arch, and my lips smash together to stifle a pleasured moan.

A raging battle springs to life inside of me. I love what he's doing, erasing the ache and pain from all the hours on my feet, but he isn't playing fair. My will to fight, stand on my own, quickly evaporates under his care.

"Ridge, I can't..." I mewl, and when his fingers press on a particularly tender spot on my heel, my eyes flutter closed. "I—"

"Shhh." Slanting his head, he leans in and captures my lips in a kiss that's hungry and demanding.

A surge of heat races down my spine, flooding my core in a flare of anticipation. I know how good we are together. The urge to touch him taunts me, and even though I know better —know where this will lead—suddenly, I can't stand it anymore.

I grab his head, fingers threading into his dark hair. My heart pumps painfully as I leap onto his lap and straddle him. His cock wedges between my legs, where I need him most.

I want more. All of him.

11

———

RIDGE

oft, ample curves fill my hands, and my head swims as Lacy's sassy mouth overtakes mine—the taste of mint and honey invading my senses.

God, she's fucking delectable.

A swell of pleasure builds within me as she rolls her hips, grinding herself against my hardening cock. Right where I want her. Where I need her.

Where I've only dreamed of having her again.

She kisses me with eagerness. It's an impassioned frenzy I've craved from the very first moment my lips met hers.

Still, I need to know...

"You want this?" I ask, breaking from our kiss. "Want me?"

Her dark eyes are hooded, cheeks tinted pink, and legs squeezed tight. She's a fruit ripe for picking, and I wait, breath held, as growing hunger wraps around me, slowly strangling the small bit of sensibility I've got left.

She pushes herself impossibly closer. Her full tits crush against my chest, and her sweet breath is hot against my ear when she whispers, "I want you inside me."

In one swift motion, I shift our balance, tearing her dress over her head and tossing it to the floor. Her bra quickly follows suit.

Smooth, sun-kissed skin greets me, inviting me to touch, kiss, and delight in the bounty of her lush beauty.

Does she know how perfect she is? What she does, not only to my body, but the rest of me as well? She's temptation and solace mixed into one natural, gorgeous package.

"Ridge," she gasps when I latch my mouth to her nipple and suck deeply.

My answering hum has her squirming over me in a way that lets me know she's ready. She's past the point of wanting, and all that's left is pure, glorious need.

Her breast comes free with a pop, and I turn my attention to the other, flicking my tongue over her sensitive peak.

"Yes." She pulls at my head, nails lightly scraping my scalp, urging me for more.

My hands find their way under her ass, and I give her breast a soft nip before I lift to standing. "Hold on."

Quick, heavy strides bring us to her bedroom, where I lay her on the bed before me, drinking in the splendor of her exquisite, turned-on beauty.

"Fuck, look at you." I run my fingers from the valley of her heaving chest, down to the apex of her thighs, where I toy with the edges of her damp panties. "So goddamn stunning."

She groans. "Please, quit looking and just fuck me already."

I can't contain my low chuckle—my girl's a spitfire. A bold, bewitching wild thing, too strong to be tamed.

And God, I love that. Both the challenge and the seduction.

"Don't worry, I know what you need. But I'm not going to fuck you." I continue teasing her with the fingers of one hand as I slide my body down between her legs, using my shoulders to push them wide. "At least, not yet."

Her panties are simple pink cotton, not meant to entice, yet the sight of them up close makes my mouth water. Or maybe that's her scent. Musky and alluring, she's appetizing as fuck.

When I kiss lightly over her cotton-covered mound, she whimpers. It's a strangled, tortured sound that makes my stomach tighten and cock twitch.

Truthfully, I want nothing more than to do exactly as she's asked—I'm dying to fuck her senseless. But there's something about controlling the sharp edge of pain that comes with holding myself back this way. It's a hedonistic adventure. One I've only ever experienced with her. One I want to experience over and over again.

Only with her.

Greedy anticipation claws at my insides, and I push aside the wet fabric of her panties and attack her pussy with my tongue.

Her surprised cry of rapture is intense, satisfying, and adds fuel to the already raging fire burning within me.

"You like that?" I taunt, fingering her deeply.

Her only response is a guttural sound of fervor, so I stroke her a little harder, a little deeper—my own urgent need to get her off matching the pace of her labored breaths.

"Yeah, you fucking do." I lick up her center once more. "You like when I own this pussy, don't you?"

Her head shakes violently, sobs of pleasure erupting from her luscious lips.

"Don't you?" I demand, slowing my movements and holding her at the edge of orgasm.

"Yes...yes, I do. Fuck, yes... Please."

The way she begs has me close to coming as well, but I tamp down hard on the sensation, before diving back in for more of her goodness.

I eat her like she's my last meal—lips, tongue, teeth, and hands eagerly devouring her. When her panties get in my way, I rip them off, not caring in the least if they're ruined.

"Oh, God," she cries when I suck on her clit, and her core clenches hard around my fingers.

Wave after wave of a pulsing orgasm rips through her—her body tensing and shaking before finally relaxing into bliss.

"Ridge?" A lazy smile graces her succulent lips, but there's a glint of something wicked and playful in her eyes.

"Yeah?"

"You still have all your clothes on."

I glance down, my gaze resisting the demand to look anywhere but at her.

"Is that a problem?" I tease, popping the top few buttons of my shirt.

"Only if you plan to keep them on."

Another pulse of arousal courses through me, and I'm filled with wonder. This woman is more than I could have imagined for myself. More than I dared ever hope for. The way I feel about her is big and scary. And the thought that maybe—just fucking maybe—she feels something too...

Well, that shit's beyond terrifying. Yet, also thrilling.

My shirt falls to the floor, my hand now hovering at my belt. "Touch yourself."

"What?"

"You heard me." The metal edge of the belt buckle digs into my palm. "Show me that you want it. Touch yourself, and I'll ditch the rest of this."

Her teeth sink into her bottom lip, and she skates a delicate hand over a breast, then lower.

A lick of fire shoots up my spine as I watch the path her hand travels, especially when she hesitates at the almost unnoticeable swell of her belly, before navigating the remaining distance to her already glistening folds.

Her fingers dance a slow circle around her clit, and she sighs.

She's the sexiest fucking thing I've ever laid eyes on. Yet, it's not the evident lust in her eyes or the slickness coating her thighs that turns me on the most.

It's the fact that she's carrying my child.

This thing I never expected—never knew I wanted—is suddenly all I can think of. *All* I fucking want. Her lushness. Her strength. Her fiery tenacity. And the marvel we've created together—the life she's growing within.

Her body is a goddamn temple, and it is well past time I worship.

"Ridge?" Her voice is a velvet fist around my cock. "You're not naked yet."

God, I love the way she toys with me.

My grin is wide and uncontrolled, and I waste no more time in losing the rest of my clothes.

Her eyes grow wide when my boxers hit the floor.

"What?" Cock in hand, I plant a knee on the bed, between her legs. "You're looking like you've never seen me before."

"It feels like I haven't." She gasps when I brace myself over her, nudging her entrance with my tip. "You're not what I remember."

I hesitate a moment, her hand still moving lightly beneath me, and my cock a single stroke away from home. "In a bad way? Or good?"

"Oh, it's good...really, really good." She smirks and then whispers, "It would probably be even better if you were inside me right now."

Wish fucking granted.

I surge forward, sliding into her tight heat, and she lets out a sharp, pleasured curse.

"How's that?" I grunt, my self-restraint next to snapping.

With her mouth slack and eyes closed, she bobs her head in surrender.

"Lace."

"Mm-hmm?"

The ache of my clenched jaw competes with my throbbing balls. I need to move. I need to move now. But more than that, I need her with me. I need to see that spark of connection in her gaze.

Roughly, I order, "Eyes on me. Now."

Her eyes snap wide, gaze catching on mine, and she lights my fucking soul ablaze.

"Good girl. Now keep 'em there."

I pull out of her, only to slam straight back home. Again. And again. And a-fucking-gain.

She moans, her lashes dipping a little, but she keeps her eyes locked on mine. It's all I can do not to come just from the depth of her emotion-filled stare.

But I'm not ready. She feels far too good to go so fast.

Lowering more of my weight onto her, I slow our frenzied pace. Still, the need to dominate her is fierce.

Gently, I wrap my hand around her neck, and my fingers caress her jaw as she tilts her head back, eyes never leaving mine, and silently gives permission. But this is it, as far as I dare take it, and already more than I can handle.

Our foreheads are nearly touching, and we breathe deeply of one another as my cock drags in and out, her core fluttering.

"I need you to come again." My voice is ragged and raw. "Think you can do that for me?"

Her answer is a whimpered plea.

My mouth seals to hers in a desperate kiss, our bodies moving in perfect rhythm. The fingers, still clamped around her neck, squeeze ever so lightly, and suddenly she's screaming into my mouth as she explodes around me.

"Fuck, you feel so fucking good. So fucking tight when you come. Fuck..."

Fuck.

I see goddamn stars as my own orgasm barrels through me.

We collapse in a heap of exhaustion, her head on my shoulder and my fingers tangled in her silken hair.

"I think you scrambled my brain." Voice sleepy, she snuggles farther into me. "But I think I liked it."

"You only *think* you liked it?"

Her laughter vibrates across my chest, lighting me up all over again.

God, this woman.

"I mean, the sex was... There aren't even words to describe it."

I wait in silence for the rest of her explanation, dreading the objections—the fucking rejection—I'm sure she's about to give.

But there's nothing.

Deep even breaths coast across my skin, and I realize she's fallen asleep.

No fucking words at all.

A sense of profound satisfaction settles over me. *Maybe I can have everything, after all.*

§

*M*orning light filters through my consciousness, waking me from one of the most restful sleeps I've ever had.

Except, instead of a gorgeous woman, a sheet covers me from the waist down.

Bolting upright, my head swivels and gaze darts around the tiny room, hoping like hell I'll find her next to me. But all that greets me is a mess of clothes, a few dingy pieces of furniture, and linens that, while clean and homey, have seen better days.

Agitation pricks at the back of my neck as I swing my legs over the edge of the bed and fish around for my boxers. Obviously, my mind was too filled with lust last night to notice how stained and threadbare the carpet is. Or to spot the cracks in the walls and watermarks on the ceiling.

God, this place is a dump.

"Lacy?" I stumble from the bedroom, taking note of all the damage—the potential goddamn danger—and realize, I'm already failing her.

Failing them both.

"Lacy." The boom of my voice echoes in the small space.

"Hush, will you?" Bleary-eyed and grumpy-looking, she turns from the kitchen sink with a glass of water in hand. "I heard you the first time."

I scan her from the messy pile of hair atop her head to the soft blue polish accenting her toes. *Still fucking exquisite.* "Everything okay?"

"Fine," she says, but the tight line across her brow makes me doubt it's the truth.

"I expected to find you in bed with me this morning." I'm testing, maybe even pushing her boundaries a little. "Or better yet, hustling to move your things to my place, so we can stay in my bed for as long as we fucking want."

She coughs and sputters on the water she's sipping. "Pardon me? Did you really just ask me to move in with you?"

"Yes, but I'm not asking. You can't stay here, Lace. This place isn't good enough for you. It's not safe."

"Are you out of your mind?" Anger—or is that excitement —flashes in her gaze. "We barely know each other. Heck, I don't even know if I like you."

"I'd say we know each other pretty fucking well, and your pussy likes me a helluva lot."

Now there's no mistaking—the look on her face is one of fury. Yet, I can tell from the way her thighs are squeezing together, my crass words have turned her on.

My dick starts rising from just the thought.

"Now you're really overstepping, and moving way too fast." She sets the glass on the counter behind her, and on sleek, supple legs, glides toward me.

An edge of restless hunger stirs within me.

"Besides,"–her voice is calm and inviting—"Chastity's already tried to make trouble with me. I don't feel like getting poked by that cactus again."

"What did she do? And why the hell didn't you tell me sooner?"

There's a glint of mischief in her gaze, and her mouth quirks at one side. "When was I supposed to tell you? Between orgasms?"

Fucking hell. "If you're not careful, I'm going to kiss the sass right off your perfect lips." How does she get me so riled up so easily?

"Promises, promises."

"Lace," I growl, fighting hard to keep my cool, "tell me what she did."

"She didn't do anything, really." Her heavy sigh washes

over me. "Just called me a whore and gave me some BS warning about staying away from you."

"That little..." My blood's boiling, but I don't want to risk turning Lacy off, not when it's so obvious I've got her turned on. "I'll talk to her."

"No need. She isn't a problem I'm worried about. She was just sizing me up...maybe trying to mark her territory...but other than lame threats, she's got no real bite. Besides, I don't need you to fight my battles."

My chest burns and heart pounds. "How's it your battle? She wouldn't even be in your life if it weren't for me. It's my mess; I'll deal with it. End of discussion."

"Your mess?" She takes a step back, lines worrying her brow, and braces herself against the kitchen counter. "Is that how you think of this? Of the baby? A mess?"

A hard growl rips from my throat, and I stalk toward her, securing her in a firm hold. "Fuck no. How could you even think that?"

She shakes her head but doesn't answer.

"You are not a burden." Frustration and a touch of anger simmer within me, but still, I'm turned on. "And I'll always take care of what is mine."

"Just promise you'll leave her alone," she says with a sigh.

Did my words even register?

She's acting like this thing's still casual. Like the second time around was charming, but not worth more...

Unless that's insecurity talking.

I grasp her chin, forcing her gaze to meet mine, and pin her with a fierce stare. "I promise. Just don't ask me to leave you alone, 'cause that's not something I'm ready or willing to do. You feel too fucking good."

Her lips part on a sharp inhale, and I sink into the feeling of her desire.

"I said you're not a burden, Lace. That I take care of what's mine. And now I'm going to prove it to you."

A look of lusty greed crosses her features, and she arches her back, giving me a wicked smirk. "And just how do you plan on doing that?"

God, her feisty attitude makes me hard all over again. "Turn around, bend over, and I'll show you."

12

LACY

"Well, dear, I know you're a hard worker, but..." Ivy-Mae Cooper wrings her sun-weathered hands and looks at anything but me. Here it comes. "Lacy, dear, how far along are you?"

Eyes on my belly, she dips her chin in the same direction, and I barely contain my sigh. Almost overnight, my baby bump became a thing.

Ivy-Mae's the office manager and hygienist for her husband's dental practice, and they need a receptionist. It seemed like a perfect fit, since I'd be off my feet, but given how she clears her throat before pursing her lips, my chances aren't looking so good.

I'd had such high hopes when she'd agreed to meet outside Oz's. Now with her question, my pregnancy literally and figuratively between us, all I want is to wrap up this dead-end chat.

"I'm in my second trimester." I could tell her the number of weeks and days like most mothers-to-be can, but I don't.

Why bother? She's annoying me and I feel judged, less than, even if I like this woman. "Just tell me why you can't hire me."

"Um, it isn't that I don't *want to* hire you. It's just that once the baby's here, I'll have to find someone else, and Dr. Cooper won't like that. We need someone long-term. It's time-consuming and stressful hiring new people."

She talks about Darnel Cooper like he isn't her husband, only the boss, and she's afraid of him. Maybe she is. Although I can't see him as anything more than a teddy bear. Oz's Club is his happy place, where he's all smiles and tips. I could challenge Ivy-Mae, tell her I'm confident that I could get Darnel to hire me, baby or not, but I doubt she'd like me saying any such thing.

Raising my hand to my brow, I shield my eyes from the setting sun. "Fine. Best of luck finding someone."

I head to the club entrance, and she mutters a feeble goodbye. My phone rings as I near the door and I pull it from my purse. Ridge.

Already exhausted and I haven't even started my shift, I'm tempted to ignore it. I'll see him later.

Since that night at my place almost four weeks ago, his sleepovers are now a regular thing. Despite mixed feelings about what we're doing, I don't hate it.

How can I when he picks me up after work, no matter how late my shift. He brings dinner if I'm too tired to cook, and while the meals are loaded with vegetables, the food is damn good.

Plus, his large, warm body next to mine in the bed every night. Arms and legs wrapped around me like he never wants to let me go. It's an indescribable comfort, and indulgence I'm desperately trying to not get used to.

But God, the way he pounds into me almost every night. All it takes is a look and he's on me. In me. And my orgasms...damn, they're deliriously violent, so much so, I forget my own name. Who knew pregnancy would make me so horny?

The shrill ring yanks me from my reverie, and I hastily answer. "My shift starts in ten minutes, why are you calling?"

I cringe at my snappish tone. Ridge isn't to blame for the rejection—Ivy-Mae's was the third this week—in my hunt for a desk job.

Seventeen weeks along and feeling every bit of it, while November's cooler weather is helping, I want off my feet. Oz's offer to find some other work for me still stands, but every time I mention it to Ridge, he shuts down the idea. For that alone, I want to stay at the club, although I'm trying to meet him halfway since he's trying too.

His gruff voice pulls me from my thoughts. "What's wrong?"

"Nothing. I'm irritable and have a long shift."

"I told you to call in sick."

His overbearing concern causes something within me to snap, and my words fire like nails from a gun. "And I don't do that kind of thing. Goodbye."

"Lace, wait. Don't get mad, but I talked to Oz—"

My muscles stiffen and a dull throbbing blooms behind my eyes. "Ridge, what the hell did you do?"

He hates me working at the club and doesn't want me to have to put up with the men and their shit. It doesn't matter that I remind him I'm not the main attraction because he reminds me that's how we hooked up. He was more interested in me than the girls on the stage.

"You had a shitty night. Don't think I didn't notice you tossing and turning last night."

Exasperated, I tilt my head back to stare at the now slate-gray sky. "I couldn't get comfortable. It's only going to get worse the bigger I get."

"I only told Oz to keep an eye on you. That you might need to take a few more breaks or—"

"Goddammit, who do you think you are?"

"I'm the father of your child."

"That's it. You aren't the boss of me." I clench my jaw at how childish I sound. "You don't get to make unilateral decisions like talking to Oz behind my back. I'm a grown woman and if I need a break, I can speak for myself. You know what? I will work at the club for the rest of my pregnancy."

Too upset to think straight, I won't mention my latest rejection from the Coopers or that whatever work I'll be doing for Oz won't be behind the bar.

"Lacy." My name's razor sharp. "I've already told you; you don't need to work—"

"I want to work. I can't sit at home and stare at the walls, and I need rent money—"

Now he cuts me off. "We've already talked about this. We're moving in together. Money isn't a problem."

"Goddammit, why aren't you listening? I don't want to be a kept woman. If that's who you want, marry Chastity."

It's a loaded shot, but Ridge is moving way too fast, and I have to slow him down. The idea of living together scares me. What if it all falls apart?

He's already dragged me to look at three places for rent, and he's talking about building a home someday. For now, his sole focus is having us under the same roof. Though Canyon Spring Ranch is his home, where he works, and most definitely in his blood, I refused to live there, and he never fought me on it. We both know living with Sage Kincaide would be a disaster.

"Fuck, Lace, I don't want anyone but you."

I suck in a breath. He's told me he wants me before— even claimed me as *his*—usually while having sex, but this time... This feels different.

We haven't talked about a future beyond finding a place for when the baby's born, and as maddening as he is with his "let's play house," a part of me likes it. I'm in awe of his protective nature and how he truly seems to want to be with me.

But I can't forget that if not for the baby, we'd be nothing to each other. Just a glorious one-night stand. Ridge is a good man and doing the right thing. That's all this is.

"Sorry." I soften my tone. "I'm frustrated. No one's going to hire a pregnant lady that's only got a few more months of work in her."

"Things didn't work out with the Coopers?"

"No. I want to work for Oz. The club and the people here are home to me. And while you may not understand it, I need to work." I rub my temple, trying to quell the dull pulse. "And if I don't get inside, Oz will wonder where I am.

See you later." I end the call before he can say another word.

Once inside, I'm shocked to see Roxy behind the bar. She isn't supposed to be on tonight.

She places a beer in front of the man at the bar and turns to me. "Hi, Lacy. Oz is in the office and he wants to talk to you."

My stomach sinks. What on earth did Ridge say to him?

"Thanks." I wave at her and saunter down the hall. "Hey, Oz." I mosey into the office and drop onto the leather sofa.

He glances up from the computer screen, his face a mask of confusion. "Thank fuck you're here. I can't figure this shit out. I've got a job for you that'll have you working in the office." Relief ghosts over his tense features. "Please take over the books. Stay on top of invoicing, revenue, and payroll. You're better at it than I am, and I hate doing that shit. You'd be helping me."

"Funny thing, I was coming to talk to you about a desk job."

He smiles. "Great, you start now. But don't worry about putting in a full day's work. An hour will do. Take some time to get acquainted with things. You can officially start next shift, and we'll figure out daytime hours for you."

I arch a brow. "And this wouldn't have anything to do with your talk with Ridge, now, would it?"

"Nah." He stands, eluding my gaze and looking uncharacteristically uncomfortable.

"Oz, I need to get paid. I can't afford to work only an hour. And if you want me in the office for nights, that's cool. Ridge doesn't call the shots."

He barks out a laugh and stares at me like I'm naïve. "You can work whenever, and remember, I promised you work out from behind the bar long *before* Ridge called. But just so we're clear, I ain't takin' on your man."

I spring to my feet. "He isn't my man."

A hard rap at the door interrupts us and the door swings open. My heart stops and nausea swirls in my stomach.

My mother shuffles into the room on shaky legs, disheveled and strung out.

Fuck my life.

I haven't seen her in months and I'm good with that, but it could be worse. Otis could be with her. At least my father isn't here.

"Hi, Oz. Could you leave us alone?" Arlene scratches at her rail-thin arm, the flesh sallow and pockmarked as her gaze lands on me. "I'm here to talk to my daughter."

"We don't have anything to say to each other," I blurt out at the same time Oz says, "Sure thing, Arlene." He looks at me long and hard. "Lacy, you good?"

My shoulders sag. "Yeah. It's fine."

The door clicks shut behind him and Arlene coos, "Hey, baby, how are you?"

"What do you want?"

"Don't be like that. Even if I didn't know you were expectin', I could tell." She points a bony finger at me, dirt embedded under her jagged, paper-thin nail. "You're glowin'. I was the same with you."

I snort, trying to ignore the bubbling wave of dread rising within me. "Spare me your lies." I sharpen my gaze to match my tone. "I'm only asking one more time. What. Do. You. Want?"

I don't like that she knows about the baby, but I'm also not surprised. Prospect is a small town, and I can no longer hide my pregnancy. Word is spreading around the club, and likely the whole damn town is talking.

The real mystery is the father and so far, no one's figured it out, although it's only a matter of time. Maybe Mommy dearest will be the first. Now *that* could be a problem.

When my parents find out the father is a Kincaide, all they'll see are dollar signs. Shit. Why didn't I think of this sooner?

"I want to help. Raising a child on your own is hard, but a baby also means a fresh start. You've always wanted out of this town. What if we left together? We'd help you raise our grandbaby." She forces her biggest and brightest smile.

"You must be fucking high. There's no way in hell I'd let you anywhere near this baby."

Arlene and Otis Hallman don't have a parental bone between them. I'd sooner leave a newborn in a lion's den than with them. They must know about Ridge, and like sharks, they smell blood in the water and aren't going anywhere until they get dinner.

"Lacy, I was a good mama, and your daddy loves you."

Vomit claws its way up my throat. How can she call Otis daddy? More like bully or abuser. She makes me sick with the pretty picture she paints of a childhood I never had.

She twirls a finger coyly around a dirty, matted clump of hair. It looks like it hasn't been washed in weeks.

"Baby girl, we'd be good for the baby. For you. We could go to Bozeman or Missoula or leave the state."

"What the hell is going on? And don't lie to me. Why are you here?"

A nervous titter skates past her dry, flaky lips and her arms fold across her middle, nails digging into her forearms. "Just listen. This is our chance to leave this place. Start over."

Shaking my head, I back away, needing to get away from her, but she grabs my arms and my blood chills at her touch. At the determined, almost maniacal way she stares at me. As if I have only one option.

Not a chance.

"Lacy, we don't got much time. Travis could come with us if you want. Think of the baby."

Vehemently, I pull from her grasp but stay close, no longer in flight mode but more determined than ever to get to the bottom of this. I don't want her to bolt when I start pressing.

"Arlene, what is this really about?"

Has Otis or Arlene seen Ridge coming and going from my place? Or Oz's? That's all it would take, especially with the news of me expecting, for them to put two and two together.

Do they know Ridge is the father and by leaving town with me, they could hold the baby for ransom in a sick, perverted kind of way?

"I can't. Otis told me not to tell you. Not yet." She thrashes in front of me as if trying to internally beat herself up.

I'm on the right track—her actions say as much—and I

gently grab hold of her shoulders to steady her. It takes several beats before she stops moving. Shit, Otis should be here, and I can't believe I'm even wishing that.

He's a bastard, but I could pressure him without worrying about him falling apart. And that's why he sent Arlene alone.

As if in a trance, she says, "I'm not gonna tell ya. You'll... You'll mess it all up."

She's prone to paranoia and can easily lose her grip on things. While I've no love for this woman, I don't want to send her over the edge, but I need a confirmation.

"Arlene, why do you want to leave town?" She cocks her head to one side, waiting for me to say more. "All your customers are here. You're established." My calm tone, and the way I talk about their drug-dealing business like it's something to be proud of makes me sick, but I'm appealing to my mother's not so practical side.

Waving her arms in the air, hands in fists, her whole frame rattles, and features tense and pucker. "Just fucking leave with us."

She repeats this over and over like a mantra, face getting redder by the second, body more unstable, and eventually, I let her go. She flees the office but not before spitting a final decree. "We'll be back. This isn't over. You're leaving with us."

My phone buzzes on the desk and my heart sinks.

Ridge: Meet me here.

Next comes an address right in the heart of Prospect—a nice little neighborhood where the homes are all way above my pay grade. Another place for us to look at and suddenly, I can't breathe.

Should I let his text go unanswered, cut ties with him

here and now? My parents will be a problem, more so when it comes out that I'm bound to the Kincaides by this baby.

And here's Ridge, itching to throw cash around and get us a home for the future when the vultures are circling.

My phone pings again, pulling me from my troublesome thoughts.

Ridge: Lace, quit stalling. I know you've read the text. Meet me now.

Involuntarily, the corners of my lips tug upward at this demanding man, and I tamp down any fluttering feelings of hope. Like always, Arlene and Otis will ruin everything.

I'll deal with Ridge now, and eventually I'll have to deal with my parents. I snatch up my phone and respond.

Me: Try again

Three bubbles dance and this time, when his response pops onto the screen, there's no containing the smile that springs to my face despite how my parents can sour things.

I have to hand it to him, he knows how to satisfy me in and out of bed, and the thought of this causes my breaths to shallow and panties to dampen. *Shit, this man.*

Ridge: Please.

13

RIDGE

*L*acy looks at her phone for what feels like the hundredth time since walking in the door. She's not only distracted and seemingly uninterested but has been giving me the cold shoulder, pulling away any time I get close.

Is it the rental?

Admittedly, the place is a bit of a dump. Built in the sixties like the rest of the homes in this area, it hasn't been updated in a couple of decades. Still, there's potential and it's not in such rough shape that a bit of cash can't fix it.

Or a lot of cash. Whatever it takes to make her happy.

Because fuck, try as I might, I have failed miserably in this regard. At least, out of bed. In the sack, my woman's satisfied...completely. And frequently.

It's everywhere else she seems troubled.

And I hate that. Not just because I feel responsible, but

because I have no clue how to change it. I thought renting a place would help—one less hardship for her to carry.

But so far, the endeavor seems useless. What the hell else am I supposed to do to set this gorgeous, challenging woman at ease?

"So? What do you think?"

Her head pops up and she tucks the phone in her purse, having the decency to at least look a bit guilty about it. "I'm not sure."

For the first time, it crosses my mind the rental might not be the problem.

Fuck, what if the problem is us? What if it's me?

"Come on, Lace." Feeling desperate—another thing I fucking loathe—I spring toward her and, grabbing hold of her hand, yank her to me. "Give it to me straight."

What looked like guilt in her expression has now turned into a lovely shade of fury. God, she's exceptional when she's mad. "I've been trying to give it to you straight for weeks. Hell...months. Ever since I first told you I was pregnant."

The hair at her nape is like silk, and I can't help but thread my fingers through it, pulling it into a tight fist.

Her head tilts back, full lips parting and eyes growing wide as she drops her purse to the floor. "What are you doing?"

"Nothing... Just appreciating the look of murder on your pretty face."

"You're impossible," she groans.

"Right back at ya, sweetheart."

"Oh, no." Her eyes narrow and my dick swells. "Do not even think about calling me by some ridiculous pet name.

I've warned you…I won't be a kept woman. And there is nothing sweet about me."

I could argue. Tell her the way she's constantly thinking of our child, putting the needs of an unborn baby ahead of her own, is the sweetest damn thing. Or that her concern for her brother and coworkers is sweeter than any of them likely deserve. Or even that she's sweet for wanting to make her own way, instead of relying on me.

But I don't.

It's all more than she's open to hearing from me. More than I'm willing to share when I don't know where I stand. A hell of a lot more talking than I want to do right now.

"Hmm." My low hum is closer to a rough growl, and it's all I can do not to rip her clothes off right here, right now. "I can think of at least one part of you that tastes mighty fucking sweet."

Her mouth drops open on a strangled protest.

"In fact, I might have a bit of a craving for it now." I slide a hand between her legs, just in case she thinks I'm bluffing.

"Ridge," she hisses, her eyes darting around the empty living room. "We can't do this here." Yet, she doesn't try to pull away or stop me when I press the heel of my hand against the growing damp spot on her leggings.

"Sure we can."

"But what if we get caught? The rental agent—what was her name?"

"Isn't coming back." I smile, the pressure in my chest intensifying along with the ache in my balls.

Was it foresight or fucking brilliance that I sent the useless and forgettable agent home with a promise to lock up when we're done? Okay...it was a promise and a few hundred dollars, but none of that matters when I've got Lacy melting in my arms and my persistent as ever cock demanding I do something about it.

She moans, her pelvis tilting and hips moving along with my touch. "What are you doing to me?"

A lick of fire shoots up my spine, feeding my growing frenzy. Or maybe that's just her—Lacy is the only fuel I ever need to stoke this burning fire within.

I lean down, my mouth at the shell of her ear, and whisper, "I'm going to do whatever I fucking want and you're going to love it. Aren't you?"

Finally, her hands are on me, frantic and full of urgent need. "Yes, yes, yes," she chants, running her fingers over my chest and pulling at my shirt. All while she continues grinding her cotton-covered pussy against the palm of my hand.

I haven't even properly touched her yet, and already she's on the edge of rapture. "I love the way you need me."

Her breath catches, hands still, and she pulls back to look me in the eye.

I meet her uncertain gaze with pure, controlled conviction. *No taking it back now.* She can't deny she needs me. At least, in this one small way.

This woman is mine. She still might not know it, but when she's in my arms, she gives herself over. Not only her body, but I think maybe a part of her soul. I feel it.

Fuck, I need it.

All of her.

But if our undeniable, hot as sin, physical connection is

the only thing I can have—if it's the only thing she ever freely gives—I'll take it. Whatever I can get.

In an instant, I capture her luscious mouth with mine, licking and sucking my way inside, while simultaneously pushing the snug band of her leggings down over her ass, to the tops of her thighs.

The hot glide of her tongue, the sharp bite of her nails, the soft sound of her moan...is all for me. All of it mine.

I tear my mouth from hers, giving a final nip to her bottom lip as though a parting gift, and slide down to my knees.

"Oh God." Her hands land on my shoulders, and she sways unsteadily on her feet.

"That's it," I urge, the lust in her gaze spurring me on. "Don't let go. Not until I tell you."

Not sure she catches my double meaning, I skim my hands up her legs and around to her bare ass, where my fingers dig into her juicy flesh. Then, on a whim, I give her a little swat.

The soft, flesh-on-flesh sound of the smack seems to reverberate in the air, competing for my attention with Lacy's sudden gasp and her eager moan that follows.

A seductive blush is spreading up her neck and across her cheeks, and she's biting her lip in a way that signals she's anxious for more but won't admit it.

So, I swat her again, this time a little harder, and a little lower...just a little closer to the crux of her thighs.

She sways, eyes closing on another intoxicating moan, and digs her fingers into my shoulders like it's all she can do to hold on.

Stunning. Simply fucking stunning.

"Eyes on me," I order with a cocky smile as my gaze dips to her belly and then farther to her glistening, wet folds. "Look at me while I eat your dripping pussy. Watch me lick it up, and make it ache for more... But don't you dare come until I tell you."

On a strangled whimper and with her eyes glued to me, she bobs her head in agreement, watching my every move.

Now this is control. This is power.

The best feeling in the entire fucking world.

Roughly, I tug her leggings down to her knees before sliding my hands back up to her ass and plunging my tongue between her legs.

She tenses, her muscles quivering in my grasp, as she slides her hands up to tangle in my hair. "Oh, my... Yes."

I push her legs apart, forcing her to widen her stance, testing the limits of her pants and her balance, and move a hand between her legs. With my mouth suctioned to her clit, I push a finger deep inside her drenched heat, stroking her from within. Then, I add another.

My eyes flick up, capturing her gaze as she pants and writhes above me.

Still, it's not enough.

A third finger joins the two already coated in her juices, stretching the silken walls of her cunt and coaxing her toward climax.

The sounds she's making are incoherent and unrestrained and a balm to my fucking soul, even as it turns me inside out.

On a growl, I drag my mouth from her fluttering pussy,

instantly missing her heady taste. "Not yet," I warn, twisting my fingers inside of her. "Don't come until I say."

This is it, the moment her boundaries are tested. The moment she truly lets herself fucking go.

Her fingers turn claw-like, breath becomes ragged, and the furrow of her brow deepens. But she keeps her eyes on me.

And she doesn't come.

My tongue shoots out, flicking a relentless pattern over her clit as I continue fucking her with my fingers, coating my hand, her thighs, and my chin with her slickness.

My cock throbs, and it's all I can do not to pull it out of my jeans and slam home inside of her...but that's not what this is about.

This is only about control. And the brilliant, delightful edge of pain that goes with it. The goddamn thrill of getting her off. Of winning her over to my dominance.

Lacy's legs are shaking now, her body straining under the pressure of her impending orgasm. "Ridge." My name is a plea—a sweet, sweet fucking song of need.

I pull my mouth from her honey, roughly demanding, "Now." And smack her ass again. Hard.

My hand comes away stinging, but it's worth it to feel the pulse of her orgasm around my fingers as waves of pressure are released.

She lets out a choked scream, overcome by the sensation, and I push back my own pleasure—my own throbbing fucking need—to watch her fall apart.

Finally, I remove my hand from between her legs and

massage deep circles over her behind and thighs as she sags into me, coming down from her glorious high.

"Good fucking girl," I murmur, wrapping my arms around her waist and kissing a soft line up her abdomen. "Always so compliant."

She stiffens again, but this time I sense there's no pleasure involved. This is one boundary she's not willing to cross —at least, not without another orgasm involved.

Not wanting to pull her out of her place of easy bliss, I nuzzle her stomach and soothe her bottom with the gentle glide of my palms. "You're the strongest, sexiest woman I know. And if I hadn't already promised you dinner, I'd be pushing to see how long I can keep you from coming on my cock."

Abruptly, I stand, pulling her panties and leggings up along with me.

She smirks, adjusting the band of her pants. "I don't remember you promising me anything. Especially not dinner, and food is one thing I never forget these days."

"I figured it was implied."

"How so?" she says through a light laugh, and I smile with her, thankful she's no longer threatening to retreat.

"Well, if I get to eat, then so do you." I wink, capturing her hand in mine before she can smack me with it, and stoop to grab her purse from the floor. "And I'm guessing it's a no on this place?"

Her shoulders rise and fall on a heavy sigh, and she scans the barren-looking bungalow, the worn wood floor letting out a loud creak as she steps to look behind her.

"It's a nice house." Her expression turns wistful, and I

wonder what the hell is going through the maze of her complex mind. I wish she'd just tell me, already.

"But it's not the right one?"

With a tug of my hand, she turns toward the door, persuading me to follow. "No, I don't think it is."

None of the places we've looked at have been good enough, and it's no wonder. I take a final look at the boring beige walls, the cheap, plastic blinds, and bare bulbs affixed to the ceiling. All the same basic, boring features as the other rentals we've seen.

If our search is only going to produce more of the same, it's time to switch tactics.

It's time I start looking to buy her something nice. Something fucking worthy of my woman and child. Maybe that'll make her happy.

Not ready to share those thoughts, I ensure the door's locked when I pull it shut. "Where do you want to eat? Walter's?"

I turn to her, coming up short when I see Chastity strolling down the sidewalk, clinging to the arm of a tall, balding man who looks like he's on his way to church, wearing a suit jacket, khakis, and loafers.

"Wow." Lacy slides her hand from mine, smoothing down a strand of hair, caught by the wind. "Someone's moved on mighty fast. Told you there was no need to talk to her."

"Found herself another sucker." I laugh. "Good for her."

Lacy eyes me with something akin to awed skepticism. "That doesn't bother you at all?"

"Why would it?" My hand finds its way back to hers, and

I tow her closer, hoping like hell she sees the truth in my stare. "She's nothing to me. Never was."

"But—"

"No, Lace, just listen. That dance you saw me share with her at my brother's wedding? That was the most intimate she and I ever got."

"Oh." Her mouth hangs open as though shocked by my admission.

"You're the only woman I want."

"Okay." She shifts away, dropping my gaze and looking back to the street, where Chastity and her new man have already passed by. "So, dinner... I was thinking we should go back to my place. I think I'd like to stay in."

A pang of discomfort tries to worm its way into my gut, but I don't allow it. She's here. She's with me. And I'm not letting her fucking go.

"Whatever you want, Lace... Whatever you want."

14

LACY

With nothing but a flimsy paper medical gown on, I shiver and clumsily climb onto the table. Ridge helps to guide me into a lying position while I try to ignore the excruciating pinch to my ready-to-burst bladder.

Why must I drink a gallon of water before an ultrasound? I'm so full that I fear I'll float away or better yet, pee right here in the exam room.

"What's wrong?" He hovers like a mother hen and squeezes the hand he's already holding too tight.

"Nothing," I grumble. It's a refrain that's become all too familiar since Otis and Arlene decided to pop back into my life.

For the last three weeks it's been nonstop texts and calls. All of them from my mother—Otis hasn't had the balls—and all of them some form of failed manipulation to try and get me to leave town.

I still don't know what they're up to, or what the heck to do about it, but I don't have the bandwidth to deal with it right now.

Now is all about my baby. Our baby—Ridge's and mine. And my aching damn bladder.

"Don't lie to me, Lace." His free hand tenderly brushes along the curve of my jaw. "You're clenching your teeth. Talk to me. Are you in pain?"

I try to hold back another kind of shiver as my insides melt at how attentive and caring Ridge has been since we got here. Instead, I end up wincing as the motion causes the prickling pressure in my bladder to intensify.

"I have to pee really badly."

Just then the technician enters the room, her neutral expression softening at my admission as she settles in front of the equipment.

"Hi, I'm Brenda and I'll be doing your sonogram. Sorry about the bladder, but we need a full one for what we're going to do today. Let's get started, and the sooner we're done, the sooner you can go to the bathroom."

"And what is it you're going to do?" Ridge's authoritative tone causes the woman to stiffen slightly and stop preparing for the ultrasound.

"Well, Mr. Kincaide." She blushes and flutters her eyelashes and I sigh, not in the least bit surprised that Ridge has this effect on her. Damn, the man knocked me up on the first go. "This is your baby's twenty week anatomy scan. I'm going to take some measurements of Ms. Hallman's abdomen and get a good look at the fetus."

"Will we be able to see the baby?" It's subtle and I doubt Brenda noticed, but I don't miss the hint of hope and, dare I say, excitement in his question.

She nods and points to the monitor. "Yes. This examination will be longer than other ones you've had, but you'll see the baby right here."

Brenda doesn't give him a chance to ask any further questions, turning to me to explain the process with the ultrasonic gel and wand.

"Okay, let's get started." She glances at Ridge. "Please understand that I'm not here to interpret the scan. That's what Doctor Anderson will do. But if you have a question about what you're looking at or if you want me to point out things, I'm happy to do so."

My fingers tighten around Ridge's palm—he hasn't let go of my hand since I put this thin gown on—and I smile first at him, reassuringly, and then at the technician. "Thank you. We understand."

He closes his mouth and watches the ultrasound wand glide over my abdomen, starting low on my pubic bone. A growl escapes him.

Brenda stalls with the wand, eyes widening. "Is everything okay?"

"Where are you going with that?" His chin points to the wand sitting close to my bikini line.

"Um..." Her cheeks flush as her mouth opens and closes a few times, and I try hard not to giggle at how absurd he's being. "In order to see the baby and all the different angles, I need to slowly move this around Ms. Hallman's stomach."

Tentatively, stealing furtive glances at Ridge, she resumes sliding the wand slowly and purposely up to my belly button.

At first, his eyes don't veer from the wand, as if he knows what's expected and plans on grading her. Once he's confident that she knows what she's doing, his sharp gaze locks on to me, cataloging my every breath and twitch as the wand glides over my belly.

A strong galloping sound fills the room, and I can't help but smile at the sound of my baby's heart.

Ridge stands and knits his dark brows together. "What is that? Is something wrong?"

This is his first time at an ultrasound, and I gently pull on his arm to get his attention.

His head swings to me, and the overwhelming adoration, clouded by the confusion and concern that swim in his blue eyes, causes my heartbeat to sputter. His genuine and unabashedly apparent love for our unborn child intensifies my joy and excitement at seeing our baby inside of me. I'm glad to share this moment with him.

Brenda beats me and says, "That's the baby's heartbeat."

Ridge doesn't look away from me as a blindingly massive smile erases any doubt or worry from his handsome face. "Wow. That's a strong beat."

I nod as a single tear, hot and happy, slides from the corner of my eye down to my ear.

Ridge softly wipes at the wet and presses a kiss to my temple. "That's our baby."

The growing ball of emotions clogging my throat only allows an, "Uh-huh," from me.

Brenda clears her throat and resumes the exam. Every so

often, she stops the wand, presses a button on the keyboard, and that's followed by a click like a camera. Tiny lines tighten around Ridge's eyes and his mouth presses into a thin line as he stares intently at the TV-like screen.

He leans over me, his free hand pointing at the screen. "Is that an arm? And the head."

Indiscernible gray-and-black blobs fill the screen, but I think he's right. That could be an arm and I can easily make out a head with a pea-sized nose.

"Yes." Brenda points at the screen. "And this is a leg." She pivots to face us both. "Do you want to know the baby's sex?"

I say no at the same time he says yes. Ridge stares down at me. "You don't want to know? Why not?"

"It doesn't matter to me." My response is more defensive than I intend, and he arches a brow.

"It's not that it matters to me—" Ridge starts to say, but Brenda interjects, as if sensing things could get heated or maybe because she's done this so many times and figures it best for us to talk about this in private.

"You two can think about it and if you want to know, Doctor Anderson can tell you." She turns back to the exam, and Ridge and I remain silent.

As much as I don't want to be, I'm bothered that Ridge wants to know the baby's gender. Why does he care? Is it about some stupid legacy and inheritance thing with the Kincaides?

"All right, we're done." Brenda cuts through my upsetting thoughts and hands me a few paper towels to wipe the gel off my stomach. "The washroom is just down the hall and Doctor Anderson should be in within a few minutes."

While Ridge attempts to grill the poor woman for details she isn't going to offer, I leave her to fend for herself. Once done, I return to the room where Doctor Anderson ambles in after me.

"Hello, Lacy. Oh." He stops short of closing the exam door to stare the man pacing the small room. "Ridge, nice to see you."

The doctor holds out his hand and the men exchange pleasantries, though Ridge cuts it short, not stopping to breathe, before stating arrogantly, "Doc, Brenda was competent and all, but she wouldn't answer any of my questions."

"In fairness to Brenda, that's what I'm here for. What do you want to know?" The doctor holds up a hand and eases over to a tall stool. "Or before that, do you want to hear what I have to say? It might answer some of your questions."

This is why I chose him. He has a way of taking control and putting even the likes of Ridge in his place without coming off rude or domineering. Ridge waves at the doctor to proceed.

"Well, Lacy, you're right where we thought you'd be in terms of gestation."

"What does that mean?" Ridge can't keep his mouth shut and I snort, which gains me a sharp, challenging gaze from him, as if to say "What? You want to know as much as I do."

He's right. I can't fault him for wanting to know everything about the baby.

"It means everything looks great. The fetus is growing and developing as it should, and there's no need to alter your due date. You're still tracking for early April. And how are you feeling, Lacy?"

"I'm good. Tired and growing." I chuckle and rub my stomach.

"Well, you look great, and your baby is doing great. Do you want to know the gender?" He looks from me to Ridge, and I wish we'd had a chance to talk before the doctor came in.

I open my mouth to respond but Ridge says, "No. As long as the baby's healthy, which is what it sounds like you're saying"—he pauses, eyes pinning the doctor to the spot until he nods—"then we don't need to know the gender." Ridge looks at me and smiles. "It'll be a surprise."

I'm sure that's the expression on my face right now. Surprise. I close my gaping mouth, not sure what happened while I was in the bathroom or why he changed his mind.

We spend a few more minutes with the doctor, then he hands us two printouts of the baby and leaves us. Ridge stares down at the black-and-white photo for far too long and I wonder what he's thinking.

"You okay?"

He snaps his head up to look at me. "What?"

"You've been silent and staring at the picture for quite a while. Is everything okay?"

"Absolutely." He carefully tucks the picture into his back pocket and snakes an arm around my waist. "Everything's perfect."

He kisses my forehead and I stare up at him. "How come you changed your mind about knowing the gender?"

I don't bother adding my fear of his potential want for a son. Isn't that what a Kincaide would want? Someone to carry on their name?

"You know me. I like to control things." My laughter bubbles from me at his admission and he chuckles. "All right. Enough of that." His finger bops the tip of my nose playfully. "I thought it would be good to know what we were having so we could plan. You know, get clothes now, decorate the nursery and all that, but…"

His pause, long and thoughtful, makes me hold my breath in anticipation of his next words. "Fuck planning. I meant what I said. All that matters is that the baby is healthy, and Lace, our baby is. And beautiful and magnificent."

"But of course—he or she is a Kincaide." It's a joke and I hold no resentment in my words.

Ridge doesn't take any offense, only nods and, tightening his grip on me, shifts so we're chest to chest. "Fuck, Lace, when that woman slid that phallic thing down, almost in between your legs." A dark cloud blankets his features for a beat. "I was ready to snap the thing in two if it went anywhere near your pussy."

I throw my head back in laughter, completely surprised by his revelation. "No. Really?"

He presses his nose to mine and rumbles, "Only I'm going in there." His hips thrust against my body, causing his hardening erection to poke my taut belly.

My thighs rub together and I'm suddenly hot and needy. Nope, we're not doing anything here, not in the doctor's office—the rental we looked at a few weeks ago was bad enough. My raging libido will have to chill.

I try to step back, but he isn't allowing any distance between us. "Uh, Ridge, the baby has to come out that way, too, you know."

"Ah…" He glances at the closed door then back to me, his heated gaze, so like a hot blue flame, scorching. "That I'll allow, but no one else. Speaking of which, my cock needs in there now."

His lips find mine, burning me once more with a searing kiss. A promise of what's to come.

15

RIDGE

"Wait 'til you see the backyard." I sweep Lacy through sliding glass doors to the large wraparound deck at the back of the house.

Mature, tall pines flank the sprawling, snow-dusted yard, and the blazing December sky ads an unplanned touch of romance to the picture-perfect view.

"Just think of it, Lace." I sling my arm over her shoulders, squeezing her closer to my side as a feeling of warmth blooms in my chest. "There's room for a playhouse and a swing, and a vegetable garden if you want one."

It's a postage stamp compared to the property at Canyon Spring, yet I can picture us here—sitting on the deck each summer night, rocking our baby to sleep in front of the fireplace in the winter, watching that child grow and thrive here, and making the space our own.

When the realtor, Sonny, first showed it to me, I thought it might be a decent fit. It's close enough to both town and

Canyon Spring to be convenient, yet far enough away for privacy. It's not so old that it needs a lot of work and not too new to lack character. Overall, a good, practical option, and at a reasonable price.

But the minute Lacy walked through the door, glowing from the cold, something changed. Maybe it was the way she toed off her boots in the foyer like she would at home, or how she rubbed at her growing baby bump each time we entered a room—her presence transformed the place. And even though her face gave no hint to what she was thinking, she looked like she fit here.

Like this sweet little house on Maple Drive was meant for her.

Suddenly I wasn't just looking at the prospect of buying a house, I was struck by a dream of making it a home. Making it *our* home.

"Hell," I continue, my vision for our future as bright as the setting sun, "we could even fit a pool back here. Or a hot tub. Or a pool and a hot tub."

Her gaze seems fixed on the horizon and the light layer of newly fallen snow, not actually taking in the sights. Has she heard anything I've said? Either she's tired or bored or…fuck, who knows what.

She's barely said a word. Our entire tour of the place has been spent with me babbling like a fool, and her either distracted or disinterested. Even our kiss hello felt a bit like a brush-off—her lips grazing mine as though an afterthought.

After all our time together, and after the surreal moment of seeing our baby through the ultrasound, two weeks ago, I thought we were past this. Beyond the need for her walls and separation.

Still hopeful, I plow on, "And that kitchen... I know neither of us is much for cooking, but it's a great space, lots of room for guests, yet cozy. Plus, four bedrooms. Sonny says it's the only place on the market with four. Normally I wouldn't trust a realtor, but he knows better than to try and screw me over."

"Mm-hmm." She turns out of my hold, sauntering back inside, and I follow like a puppy at her heels.

"He says it'll go fast, so if you like it, I'm thinking we should put an offer in tonight. Tomorrow at the latest."

She seems to wander aimlessly, running a hand over the granite countertop as she passes through the kitchen, her sock-covered feet moving silently over the hardwood. In the center of the room, she pauses before turning in a slow circle with her gaze stuck on the floor.

Finally, she stops to face me. Her head is bowed, one hand cradling the captivating swell of her belly, and a thick lock of hair trails over her shoulder, curling around the plump curve of her breast.

She looks subdued. Submissive. Like she belongs here, pregnant and...mine.

All fucking mine.

"You haven't said much." The strain in my voice seems amplified by the small space. "What do you think of it?"

"Ridge..." My name's followed by a heavy sigh that squashes not only my raging libido, but most of the hope I've been carrying as well.

I should have expected her to object—she's been fighting

this move every step of the way from the moment I first suggested it. If it's not the size or the location, it's some other worry. There's always an excuse. Always a reason to stay where she is. Always something to block me from doing what's right. From making her well and truly *mine*.

She says she doesn't want to be a kept woman, like I'm planning to lock her up and throw away the key. Like I want anything for her other than the best.

With all her stalling, I've got to wonder if her reluctance isn't so much about the place as it is me. Because even though we've spent nearly every available hour together these past two months, and despite feeling closer to her than any woman I've ever met, she's still not truly *with me*.

I can make her come on my cock, repeatedly, and some-times with only a single stroke, but no matter what I say or do, I can't seem to win her trust. And I can never tell what she's got going on in that quick-witted mind of hers.

Does she even want to be here?

"You don't like it?" I ask, dancing around the truth and avoiding my fears.

With a huff, her hands land on her hips, and her dark stare collides with mine. "What's not to like? Granite, hard-wood, four bedrooms, and that clawfoot tub in the second bathroom? It's stunning. More beautiful than anything I could ever imagine owning."

"But?"

"As always, it's too much," she says with another sigh, as though talking about the future—our future—is too big a demand.

"It's not *that* much, Lace, and we need to do this before

the baby comes. You'll want to get the nursery set up, and you can decorate however you want—any room. Hell, every room."

"And once again, you're not listening to me." Her sudden sharpness steals my breath. "I said it's too much. I meant it's *too much*. It was bad enough looking at rentals, but buying a place...buying *this* place... I can't afford to pay for half of it. Heck, I can't even afford the tub."

Money. I should have known. It always comes down to money with her.

"I don't expect you to pay for any of it. I can afford it. I told you I take care of what's mine. Why won't you just let me take care of you like you deserve?"

She growls—actually fucking growls—like a feral beast. Her teeth are bared, and her eyes flash murder. She's wild, incensed, the sexiest fucking thing I've ever seen...

And so far from being on the same page as me, it's painful.

"For the last time..." She pads forward until she's close enough to jab her finger to my chest. "I do not need you or anyone else to take care of me."

Each word is punctuated by a stab of that single, delicate digit, and it slowly shreds my heart. "What I deserve is for you to respect my wishes and quit throwing money at me like it'll solve all your problems. Just because you've got the cash doesn't mean you need to flaunt it all over the place, and especially not around me."

All my problems? *Flaunting*? "What the hell are you talking about?"

Her lips mash together in a tight line, and she withdraws, attempting to skitter backward, away from me. "Nothing."

Like lightning, I'm on her, catching her around the middle. With her arms trapped between us, I crush her body to mine. Soft, sensuous curves mold to me, and despite her reluctance and the dread brewing in my belly, I'm instantly hard.

My lips itch to claim hers, ravishing until she yields. To taste the lust as it burns between us, and coax the truth from her petulant mouth.

God, what this woman does to me.

On a deep breath, I inhale her rousing scent and attempt to calm my jangling nerves. "I need you to look me in the eye and tell me the truth."

In pure Lacy fashion, she does the complete opposite of what I've requested and closes her eyes. She squeezes them tightly, wincing as though the truth is too harrowing to even consider.

"Tell me." My voice is a razored demand—too harsh, too urgent, too late to take it back.

Now her eyes snap open, the dark orbs pinning me in a defiant glare. "You have no idea what it's like to come from nothing. To be so close to the bottom there's nowhere left to fall."

My arms tighten around her, the truth I so desperately wanted tugging at my possessive heart.

"Do you know how impossible it is to climb your way out of that?" she asks. "Especially when the people you're leaving behind want nothing more than to pull you back down to rot with them?"

"You think I've never been dragged down by others?"

"It's not the same." Her voice softens to barely a whisper, but it's still laced with cynicism. "You'll never understand."

"Not if you don't give me the opportunity to try." I shift my hold, cupping her face and stroking my thumb along the temptation of her plump bottom lip.

Her eyes narrow on me, but I refuse to wither under her fierce gaze. "I want to understand. There's nothing I want more than to make your life easier—to take care of you and our baby. But if you keep locking me out like this, pushing me away instead of explaining... You're not giving me a chance."

This time her sigh sounds a bit like defeat, yet the crease of her brow only intensifies. "I had an unexpected visit from my mother a few weeks ago, and she's been calling and texting me ever since."

"Okay? And that's a bad thing?"

"As if you don't already know. All of Prospect knows what lowlifes Otis and Arlene Hallman are. Hearing from either of them is never good."

The knot in my stomach twists. "I'm sorry, Lace. I honestly didn't know. I mean...sure, I've heard rumors, but I don't put much faith in the validity of the Prospect gossip mill."

"Well, you're about the only one." Her voice wavers slightly, but her body remains rigid in my hold. "The rest of town treats it as gospel, but in this case, they're right to. Arlene and Otis aren't good people, Ridge, and I can't remember a time when either of them was sober or even tried to be. I've spent most of my life working to step out of their dark shadow."

Shit. Things finally start clicking into place—her desire to stand on her own two feet, refusing my help, and her worry about being a burden. Despite knowing exactly who Arlene and Otis are, what they do, and how deeply despised they are by most of the folks in town, I never stopped to consider how much of their shit would blow back on Lacy.

Or how much hurt she'd be carrying around because of it.

This trauma runs deep—at least, much deeper than I realized—and here I've been pushing her, practically forcing her to do things my way. Fuck, I really am a controlling asshole.

"So, she wanted something from you, I'm guessing."

Her eyes drop to my chest, where her hands are curled into tight fists. "They always want something, but this time she's offering me something. She knows about the baby, and she said they want to take me out of town. A fresh start—"

"What the fuck?"

She jumps at the boom of my voice, and my first instinct is to hold her closer. Only, with my blood boiling and mind swirling the way it is, I can't stand still.

Releasing her, I pace to the back door, seeking the peace of that beautiful view, but the sun has disappeared behind the mountains, and clouds are rolling in to cover the stars. The magic is gone—broken by the confusion and doubt her words have caused.

"Is that what you want? A fresh start, without me?"

I watch her reflection in the glass as she stares at the floor again, her head shaking. "I... I don't..."

Her uncertainty cuts, deeply.

This woman is so confident and strong, and she never backs down. To hear her faltering now, just when I thought maybe we were getting somewhere, and all because of her miscreant parents... Well, it breaks my fucking heart.

I turn on my heel and stalk back to where she stands, now watching me with tears swimming in her eyes.

"What did you tell her, Lacy? What do you want?" I can't help the apathy that seeps into my tone—it's that or rage, and no way in hell am I taking this shit out on her.

"I wanted to tell her it would be a cold day in hell. But you're missing my point here. They're up to something."

Another obstacle. Only, this one is more than an excuse, more than a roadblock. This one feels a hell of a lot like a threat.

"Like what?" I ask, trying but failing to sound calm.

"I'm not sure, exactly, but if they've figured out the baby's yours... Ridge, I'm afraid of how far they'll go and what they might be willing to do to somehow profit off this. Off the baby."

The urge to do violence courses through me—overwhelming and dangerous. Am I shaking? "Not happening. I'd die before I let them or anyone—"

"This is why I didn't tell you." She crosses her arms protectively over her stomach, like she can physically shield our unborn child from my wrath. "I knew it would only upset you, and I'm more than capable of dealing with it myself.

Arlene and Otis are my problem, not yours. And I would never go anywhere with them."

Her eyes dart to mine, hesitant and seeking. "I want to stay with you."

"Okay, then." I reach out to her, but my fingers only brush down her arm as she pulls away.

"So, you're going to drop all this and let me handle it?"

"No fucking way."

"Ridge—"

"No. I'm sorry, Lace, but this isn't only about you. This involves our baby, which means by default it involves me. I promise I'll protect you, and my last name won't cause you any harm."

"You already promised me that but your Mama, then Chastity, and now this. I don't know what to believe." The intensity of her words is only rivaled by the hard set of her mouth and the steel of her spine.

There she is—the stubborn, sexy, hardworking woman I can't get enough of. It's nice to see her confidence back. I only wish she wasn't so steadfast in her refusal of my help.

"Lacy, please." This time when I reach for her, she doesn't sidestep me.

My fingers tangle in the hair I'm so obsessed with, and I revel in the feel of the silky strands as they glide over my skin. "I've never lied to you. Never hidden anything from you and I never will."

My breath stalls, throat tightens, and I almost choke on my next words. "If you can't learn to trust me, I don't know how this relationship is going to work."

"Relationship?"

Anguish slices through me at the single word. Not because it's a question, but because of the panicked look on her face.

"I agreed to give you a chance to be in your child's life. You and I..." she trails off.

"You and I what? What exactly do you think this is? We're sleeping together. I stay at your place all the time, and we're looking to move in. We're having a baby together for fuck's sake. If that's not a relationship, what the hell is it?"

Her mouth drops open, and her eyes widen. "This is all moving way too fast, that's what it is. Sleepovers, dealing with family, buying a house..."

My insides twist as I wait for her next words, thoughts of our dream house—dream life—crumbling.

"We haven't even been on a date."

Well, fuck.

16

LACY

"*I* saw Arlene today." Travis chews on the toothpick dangling from the corner of his mouth and my heart rate doubles its pace.

"Oh. Did you talk to her?"

"Nah. She was with some guy, never saw him before, and as soon as I called out to her, they took off like cockroaches scurrying from the light."

"Huh. I wonder what that's all about. What do you think she's up to?"

He scratches the dark scruff on his chin and narrows his gaze on me. "Why the hell do you care?" I shrug in a feeble attempt to downplay my interest, and to avoid eye contact, I busily clean the bar top. It's no longer my job and given the side-eye Roxy lobs my way, she's saying as much. She has my old shift while I now work days in the office, and already have the hang of things.

"She knows about the baby. I just want to test the waters."

I fold the damp cloth and place it on the counter as I shoot Roxy an apologetic smile. "See if I have anything to worry about."

It's been over a month since I saw Arlene, and although she hounded me for a few weeks after that visit, she's now gone silent. Which, if I'm being honest, puts me even more on edge.

I've considered talking to her, even to Otis. To confront them about their intentions because as conniving as they are, neither of them can keep their mouths shut. With the right prodding, they'd spill their stupid yet devious plans. Then I'll know what I'm dealing with it.

But on my own, it's a risk, and although I've thought about asking Travis to be my backup, I won't drag him into this mess. Not unless I have to.

"What do you..." He stops midsentence, his features hardening as he works it out. "Fuck, you worried about what they'll do when they find out Kincaide's the father?"

What he doesn't say, though it's written on his face, is that there's no way they don't already know, not in this town and given how far along I am.

I swallow with difficulty, trying to get past the eventuality. "Yes and no. I want to cut them off before they become a problem. That's all."

"Let me..." He pauses, gaze sharpening on something behind me and then down to my middle as a solid arm slides around my waist.

A subtle hint of leather and spice hits my nostrils before I feel the heat of Ridge at my back. Instinctually, I melt into him, ease settling over me.

"Lace." His strong hand rests gently on my swelling belly. "You ready?" He kisses my temple and I nod. "Travis."

My brother's cheek muscle tics, jaw clenching. "Ridge." He slides off the stool and pulls the toothpick from his mouth. "Lacy, I'll talk to you later." Then he glances down to the bar. "Roxy, Lynette, see you, ladies."

They sweetly call after him and I rub at the center of my chest, wishing the pinch of distress away. Travis has accepted Ridge will be in my life, and his to a lesser extent, but he still doesn't like it. I'm not sure he ever will.

"Talk later, T." I spin to face Ridge. "I'm starving."

"Good because I've got a surprise for you, and it involves food."

"Yes." I beam and let him lead me out of the bar to his truck as my head swims with thoughts of my brother, Ridge, my parents, and how or if I can control any of what may come.

After we saw the house on Maple Drive less than two weeks ago, Ridge put in an offer. Despite there being a counteroffer—and probably because his name is Kincaide—we got the house.

Reluctantly, I told Travis I was moving in with Ridge, bracing for the worst, but he had nothing to say, which in some ways was worse. Even in his silence, it was plain to see Travis wishes things were different. That we didn't have to get into bed with the Kincaides.

Well, bro, it's too late for that. I'm sleeping with one on a regular and, if Ridge has anything to say about it, permanent basis.

In the beginning, when I'd first found out I was pregnant,

the regret had been real and overwhelming but now, I can't say the same. And while it hurts to see my brother wrestling with that reality, I've no doubt he'll put his issues aside for the sake of my child.

And despite my hesitations, Ridge's excitement about the house and our future is contagious. There's no denying I love the house. What's not to love? It's better than anything I'd ever hoped to live in. Too much even, and that's what scares me the most.

Forget the possibility of our union eventually imploding, we could have bigger problems. Otis and Arlene are already up to something. What happens when they see the house? See me living with Ridge Kincaide? They'll be on us, demanding money all the time. I've got to deal with them fast.

Ridge's voice tugs me back to the moment. "Sonny called earlier today. The inspection went well. No issues with the house, and the seller has agreed to our closing date. The place will be ours before New Year's."

"Really?" I gape at him, head spinning with how fast all of this is happening, though I shouldn't be surprised. "I don't even know what to say."

The truck stops in front of a park only a street away from our soon-to-be new home.

He turns to face me. "Are you happy?"

His question throws me for a loop. Am I happy? Strangely, until this moment, I haven't given it any thought.

From a young age, I learned not to hope for things that most people take for granted. And happiness? Well, that wasn't ever important. Only the necessities of survival mattered.

"Lace?" He cocks his head to one side and squeezes my knee. "Answer me. Please."

"Uh, yeah, I am." With each word, my smile grows, throwing me more and more off-kilter. "I am happy." Glad to be seated, I laugh, realizing otherwise I might be on my ass.

"Good." He shuts off the engine and before I can say a word, he's out of the truck and opening my door.

"Why are we at a park?" Taking me by the hand, he leads me toward an area where the grass is now covered in a white blanket of snow. "I thought you were taking me for dinner?"

"We can eat now if you want. Uh..." He pauses and awkwardly scratches at the back of his neck.

When he looks at me again, he's blushing, and I nearly trip over my feet at the shocking sight. What is up with him?

"Ridge, are you okay?"

"Yeah. I thought this was a good idea and now it feels..." He scans the near empty playground, then a small frozen patch of what I'm guessing is meant to be an ice rink, where a young boy is sliding. "This is stupid and I should've—"

I grab his glove-covered hand and tighten my grip. "Hey, I'm sure this isn't stupid, but can you explain it to me?"

He threads his fingers through his dark hair, and his eyes lock with mine. "I wanted to take you on a date. When you mentioned it a couple of weeks ago, I was pissed that I hadn't thought of it, and then I wanted it to be right...perfect."

A slow smile skates across my lips and I nod encouragingly, wanting him to know that I'm with him and want to hear more.

"I know it's just a park and it's cold out here, but soon enough, this will be our life, and that's why I chose it. I wanted us to check the playground out together before the baby comes."

My heart warms and a huge smile overtakes my face. Never have I seen Ridge look so young, even boyish, and somewhat unsure, but oh, so sincere.

"It's a great idea. Kind of like we get to be a kid one more time before our child arrives." My hand goes to where the buttons on my coat are pulling around my stomach, and his gaze dips with my motion.

"Yes. Now you said you're hungry. Let's eat first and then we can play." He leads me to a small wooden structure, no bigger than a shack, and I'm surprised I didn't notice it before.

Once inside, I'm hit with warmth and the sweet smell of wood and spice.

"What is this?" A small bistro table for two sits in the center of the tiny shack, with a window on one wall, looking out at the park.

It's rustic and cozy with blankets and cushions on each chair and a basket on the table, and it's all themed for a country-style Christmas.

"If the weather was warmer, I'd have gone for a picnic in the park, but since it isn't, I figured we could picnic indoors."

"Is this shed always here?" Even as I ask, I know the answer.

"Ah, no. It's temporary. I had it put up so you wouldn't be cold."

Before I can do any more than gape at his extravagance—

I can't even imagine how much this would have cost and what it would take to arrange all of this—there's a knock on the door.

It's a delivery guy with food from The Railway, the best burger joint in town.

Ridge motions for me to sit down. He slides one of the woolen blankets on my lap and over my legs and I laugh, looking up at him. "Damn, you're good."

The smell of the food causes my stomach to gurgle. He chuckles and sits down next to me. "I better feed you."

We dig into our burgers and fries. They're cooked to perfection and not a vegetable in sight—well, unless you count the lettuce and tomato on the burger.

"Wow, that was good and just how I like it." I wipe the napkin across my mouth.

"Good. Oz may have helped by letting me know your favorites. He talked me out of something more formal. I mean, I figured since it was nearly Christmas... But he was right. This was better."

"You did good." I take a sip of my chocolate milkshake and marvel at the idea of Ridge not only seeking advice from Oz, but actually listening. Maybe he's not always as control-driven as I thought... Or maybe it's just that he cares about getting this date right.

"Do you want to sit here for a bit or maybe walk around outside? I'd suggest the swings or something else..." He waggles his brows suggestively. "But that might be too cold."

"Let's chill on the swings."

He chuckles and pulls me outside. We both shiver as the crisp wintry air hits us. We sit side by side on the swings, holding hands, and pump our legs in tandem. We're not aiming to go high or fast, just content to sway back and forth. A light icy breeze drifts over us as the December sun slowly sets in the sky.

I shudder and tighten my scarf around me.

"You cold? We can go." He slows his swing and I shake my head.

"No. It's fine. Let's stay for a few more minutes."

He glances sideways at me tentatively. "Have you heard any more from your mother?"

Is he making conversation or also worried about my parents?

"No and I'm no longer concerned about it." While not entirely true, I plan to handle them and don't need Ridge going all Mister Fix-It on me.

A blond boy, maybe five or six, the same one I saw gliding across the ice, scurries over to us, facial features scrunched up in consternation. "Hey, mister, what are you doing here?"

Ridge smiles down at him and settles his feet flat on the ground. "We're swinging."

The boy plants a hand on his hip and narrows his gaze at us. "But you're too old."

"I don't think so." Ridge chuckles and glances at me with a twinkle in his eye, clearing enjoying this exchange. "You're never too old to swing and we like it. Don't you?"

"Yeah, sure, but I'm a kid." He puffs out his chest and shakes his head at Ridge like he's clearly out of touch. "My mom says I can't play in the park in the winter, but I like it. My favorite is the slide. Do you wanna try it?"

He points at the green, plastic structure, maybe six feet

tall, as if we might be too old or stupid to know what a slide is. I burst out laughing and the boy wrinkles his nose at me, clearly not amused.

Ridge pulls on my hand and in a teasing tone asks, "Sure, but aren't you worried we're too old?"

The boy doesn't bother with a response. He's already at the base of the ladder and effortlessly scales the frosted steps before whizzing down what I'm sure is a freezing slide. He's showing off and we indulge him, both of us *oohing* and *ahhing* in amazement.

"Now, your turn." He points to me, tone skeptical as if he can't wait to see just how wrong I do it.

Ridge hesitates, tugging on my hand until I look at him, expression concerned. "It's icy. I don't think..." His gaze lands on my stomach and the unspoken question—is it safe for the baby—lingers between us.

I'm not wild about the idea but think I can do it. I'll take my time and won't be reckless.

"I'll be fine." I whisper not wanting the boy to hear and give him another reason to think we're old, clueless adults. "Hang on to me."

I wink and he takes my direction to heart. Ridge holds my waist as I climb up the few steps of the slide. Before I'm even firmly seated at the top, he races around to stand at the bottom, arms outstretched, muscled thighs braced to catch me.

It's in this moment, I'm hit with the strangest of feelings. A warmth and understanding washes over and through me. He's so protective and loving in his overbearing way.

This is how he'll be as a father.

He jokes with the boy about how he's not sure if he can do it. The slide might be too high, and I watch from my perch, overflowing with an unnamed emotion.

Definitely affection and admiration, but also something different...something more.

Ridge Kincaide will be a good father.

"Hey, lady, are you coming down or what?" The boy fidgets impatiently and blows out a puff of white air.

I push off, giggling and smiling, as I swoosh down the slide. It's freezing and my teeth chatter. Before my feet can hit the ground, Ridge scoops me into his arms and his lips press against mine.

The boy makes a loud gagging sound. "Yuck, you're gross."

He runs from the park and down the street as we pull apart laughing.

A little breathless, I rest my forehead against his neck. "That was fun."

"Yeah, it was." Keeping me close, he walks toward his truck. "You cold? Let's get you warmed up."

He pulls me into his side in the back seat of the truck. It's warm and comfortable in his arms. My head rests on his shoulder, and I stare out the window at the darkening purple sky. "What are you doing to me?"

He pauses in rubbing the side of my arm. "What do you mean? You didn't like our date?"

Though I can't see his expression, I detect the uncertainty in his tone and shake my head. "Best damn date I've ever had."

"That's what I like to hear."

"Though, I doubt I'll ever have another date build a shed for me."

"Lace, I'll do whatever it takes. Move mountains, cause floods." He's joking as his voice booms then he drops his tone to something more suggestive and intimate. "Besides, if you don't know it by now, we aren't in any way conventional."

I lift my head to look at him. "Does that bother you?"

"No fucking way. Who says we have to do things the way everyone expects? That isn't who we are. Fuck the rules and expectations. We make our own way." His hand lovingly rubs my belly. "You and me and baby."

"Ridge, thanks for an amazing date." Unable to resist, I run a hand through his hair.

His eyes shutter briefly, then he tightens his grip on my waist. "Glad you liked it."

"No, like isn't the right word. I loved it."

Twilight settles around us, and I can't help but feel understood. Our date proves I haven't given him enough credit. He knows me. Some might say a date at a park, in the winter no less, isn't a date at all.

They'd be wrong.

Despite the lengths he went to put the shed together so we'd be warm, he also took the time and care to do something I'd enjoy, that will mean something to us, to our future.

I'm not comfortable with fancy restaurants, expensive meals, or even the people. There's enough hustle and bustle at Oz's, and I tolerate it because I have to. But tonight, this date, the solitude, and even our fun with the boy, it was all simply perfect.

More and more he's proving to me how right we are

together. How our baby will have two loving parents who like each other, heck, more than like.

If I'm not careful, I could easily come to depend on this man—to love him—and that scares me to death because there's so much working against us. What happens if we drift apart or in the long run, don't work out?

An odd rolling sensation prickles up my spine and my chest constricts. Ridge Kincaide could easily be my ruin.

17

RIDGE

"**S**tay." Lacy moves backward through her apartment door, beckoning me to follow.

I prowl toward her, but only close enough to land a kiss on her rosy cheek, still chilly from being out in the cold. "I told you; I never have sex on a first date."

Laughing, she licks her lips, pops the buttons on her coat, and uncoils the scarf from around her neck. "I promise I'll make it worth your while."

Fuck, she's tempting, but it would be too easy to screw this thing up right now. Everything between us is still so tender and new, and my heavy expectations for our future have already risked crushing it all.

The reality of our situation hit home for me when we first viewed the house on Maple—*our house*. Lacy's like a new foal. She's skittish and wary, especially around the topic of our relationship. And there I was, rushing us into home ownership when we'd never even gone on a date. It's no wonder she was so goddamn hesitant.

This evening, though... Damn, it was near perfection.

Something special's happening between us. We're forming a bond like I've never experienced before, and I want her to know it. She needs to understand, this is more than sex.

In bed, we're explosive—a tinderbox waiting to ignite. So amazing, I'll always want more. But what's the use of this constant craving if my intensity scares her off? Slowing us down is the only sensible solution.

"Please, Ridge."

My cock is painfully hard, and hearing her beg only makes it worse. Is she trying to torture me?

Unable to resist, I lean in and kiss her for real, my tongue delving into her mouth, claiming it the way I crave to claim the rest of her. All of her.

She responds immediately, grasping onto the front of my coat like a lifeline, and moans into my mouth.

God, it would be so easy to get lost in her right now. To give in to my body's constant demand for more.

But waiting only adds to the thrill. That heady combination of pleasure and pain I can't seem to get enough of with her.

The ecstasy of being in control.

I break away from her, using both my physical and mental strength to put distance between us. "Goodnight, Lace."

The sound of her objection is a strangled cry of frustration that soon shifts to laughter when I turn and walk away.

Back home in my office and still high off the success of our first date, I struggle to find something productive to do. Preferably something that will take my mind off the fact that I just left my woman standing unfulfilled at her front door.

Except, the work on my desk is minimal and a bit useless, as far as distractions go. I'm about to wrap it up when there's a light tap on the open door and Mama pokes her head in.

"Oh Ridge, I'm so happy you're finally here." Her oddly sweet tone and painted-on smile have me immediately on guard. "It's been so long."

"You saw me only a few days ago." I lean back in my chair, folding my arms over my chest, taking her measure.

She sashays her way into the room, uninvited. "I know, but we haven't had a chance to talk, and I miss that."

A chill finds its way up my spine, and like a roped steer, I've got no way out. Normally, it wouldn't bother me one bit, but then I'd usually be on her good side. Now, with this silent battle we're waging, I have no idea which way things will go.

From the look on her face, she already believes she has the upper hand.

I hide my smile, knowing she's got a whole heap of disappointment coming her way.

"It's getting late." I shut off my computer and stand, making it clear I'm not up for any of her games. "If you want to chat, maybe it can wait until daylight."

Her eyes narrow but her voice is still sweet as honey when she asks, "Can't you spare five minutes to update me on your life?"

"You already know what's going on, Mama. There's nothing more to tell."

"That's not what I've heard." Her phony smile grows wider. "According to Sonny Cohen's office, you're looking to buy yourself a house. Or should I say, you *tried* to buy a house for your mistress? Too bad that didn't work out."

Mistress? The way she says it makes Lacy sound like something to be hidden. A dirty little secret I should be ashamed of.

Dark spots start to form at the edges of my vision, but as furious as she makes me, nothing can dispel the giddy high I'm riding. Mama thinks she's played me—thinks she already won—and I can't wait to burst that bubble.

"Her name is Lacy, and either you call her by it, or you don't mention her at all. I won't tolerate you trying to demean her. As for the house...I figured you might try something."

She opens her mouth to interject, but I barrel on. "Don't bother trying to deny it. I know you too well. But you forget, I've got all the same connections and clout as you. Hell, maybe more, since I'm the one you chose to represent you so often."

Some of the color drains from her face, her bravado slipping with it.

"Despite your best attempts to interfere, the house is mine. Mine and Lacy's. You've lost, Mama. In so many ways."

"Well..." She clears her throat but doesn't seem to back down. "Congratulations, I guess."

"Now you want to say those words?" I ask through a bitter laugh. "Not when it matters, but when you're forced to accept defeat... I don't get it. Why can't you mind your own damn business and just be happy for me?"

"Mind my own business?" Oh, now I've poked the bear. "Don't be ridiculous, it's all my business. You of all people should understand."

She makes a tsking sound, as though I'm a testy child. "When your father died, it became *my* responsibility to carry this family. And after all the years I stood by him, cleaning up his messes and pushing him to greatness, do you honestly think I'd allow his legacy to be tarnished?"

"Tarnished? How? By me buying a house, starting a family, and doing what he, and most others, would consider the right goddamn thing?"

More like because I'm choosing happiness over obligation.

"Don't take that tone with me." She huffs, turning her nose in the air like she's the authority on all that is right in the world.

Or at least, everything in my world. With her head held high and voice full of superior conviction, she says, "You'd have nothing if it weren't for me."

A heavy ball of burning tension forms in my gut. "You make it sound like I've had everything handed to me. Like I haven't studied, planned, and worked...fucking sacrificed." The breath sawing in and out of my lungs is like sandpaper.

Still, I go on, "If I left it up to you, I *would* have nothing. No lightness. No happiness. No love. And I'm sure if you didn't need me to run this place, you'd strip me of Canyon Spring Ranch too. Hell, I'm surprised you haven't tried to oust me from this family the way you did Brooks."

Her smile falters, her mouth falling slack, and she seems at a loss for words.

Well, there's a first.

"Look," I say, my jaw aching from how hard I've been clenching it. "I know you only want what's best for me—for all of us—but you need to loosen the reins. I'm not giving up my birthright and will always do what's best for this business, but that does not include giving up Lacy."

"But those people—her awful family. They can't be trusted."

"Her parents have nothing to do with this," I boom. Why is this still a topic of conversation? And how the hell do Arlene and Otis Hallman keep getting in my damn way?

"She's done everything in her power to get away from them." My voice is still too loud, too harsh, but she needs to get this message.

It's now or never. "She wants to do better. To be better. And she is. She's the hardest working, most honest damn person I know. But fuck, the way you and everyone else in this town automatically lump them together is why she's been so hesitant to let me in her life—in *my child's* life."

Mama's eyes are wide, and she clutches the strand of pearls around her neck. If I didn't know better, I'd say she looks guilty. But Sage Kincaide has never felt a shred of remorse in her life.

"Lacy is going to be a great mom, and if I'm lucky, she'll let me try to be a decent dad. I want her in my life, so she's staying, and that's nonnegotiable."

"I had no idea you felt this way." Her voice is a near whisper, and the pool of liquid at the corner of her eyes looks an awful lot like tears. "You feel strongly for this girl."

"Yes, I do."

Absently, she nods, still twisting the beads in her hand.

Maybe I've said too much? Pushed her too far? But damn, it had to be said.

When she finally speaks again, her voice is strong and unbroken. Whatever emotion I saw—real or an act—has been brushed aside, replaced with her usual bluster. "In that case, I think there's something I should tell you—something I can help you with."

"Okay?" The knot in my gut pulls tighter.

Do I trust her?

Fuck no. But that doesn't mean I don't need her—or at least, her merciless strategies.

"I know how to get rid of her parents."

❧

The faint smell of rotting garbage permeates the air, growing stronger the closer I get to the Hallmans' trailer home. My nausea grows stronger too, my already twisted insides revolting against this decision.

I shouldn't be here. Not after the promise I made to Lacy. Not when things between us are finally coming together.

But what other choice do I have?

I can't pretend these vipers aren't slithering around, waiting for their moment to strike. And I sure as hell won't leave my pregnant woman to deal with the aftermath of a mess she didn't create.

When Mama told me what she'd done—how she'd offered Arlene and Otis money to leave town with Lacy—I just about lost my mind.

Of all her schemes and dirty deals, this one takes the

cake. Not because of how utterly ruthless it was of her, but because I'm the one she stabbed in the back.

Me. The person who held her up when Clay left home. The one who kept her abreast of all the lies Pa told. The guy who helped push his own brother out of the way... The only one who knows her deepest, darkest secrets.

And after I'd already talked with her, made my position clear, and she'd already agreed to leave well enough alone.

Still, as furious as I am, I can't say I don't understand.

She believes in family first, which most would agree is a positive and honorable motto. Except Mama's lost sight of the meaning.

For her, it's become more about the perception of family rather than the reality. She believes it's her duty in life to make us look good. To keep up appearances and continue elevating the family name in society.

She wants us next to God.

Hell, she'd *make* the Kincaides all gods if she could. Nothing but the best will do for her children. But only if she's controlling things behind the scenes.

I just wish she understood I'd rather be happy than simply appear to be. What's the point in having it all if it makes you fucking miserable in the end?

So here I am, at the threshold of what feels a little like hell on earth, about to make a deal with these snakes. Only, in this scenario, I might be the one who's the devil.

With the brim of my hat pulled low and my hands in tight fists, I rap my knuckles against the trailer door.

For a moment there's only silence. I'm about to knock

again when the sounds of panicked scrambling and hushed shouts of anger reach me.

They argue briefly about whether to answer, and then more vigorously over which one of them will do it.

I'm ready to break the damn door down when finally, a frenzied-looking woman answers. Arlene.

Stringy hair, glassy eyes, and arms covered in scabs and scars. She shifts from foot to foot, twitching as though performing some freakish sort of dance.

If her addiction were any more obvious, she'd be carrying a sign.

"Whatcha' want?" Despite her frantic appearance, her words are slow and slurred.

"No, Arlene, the question is... What do you want?"

"Huh?"

Otis plows his way to the door, the entire trailer shaking with the pounding of his heavy, stumbling stride. "Who is that?"

"I think it's Ridge Kincaide," Arlene says, her head whipping from me to her husband and back again. "That's you, right? Lacy's baby daddy?"

I nod once, keeping my face a blank mask.

"That's him," Otis says, peering at me from over his wife's head.

"Otis, Arlene." Their names are like barbed wire in my mouth, but I remain as pleasant as can fucking be. For now. "I'd like to offer you a deal."

"Deal?" Otis pushes Arlene aside, and puffing out his chest, looks me in the eye with his hollow, dead stare.

Is there any humanity left in this man? Or are these two

driven by nothing more than the hungry need for their next fix?

With their wild looks and uneven temperaments, combined with whatever drugs they've got running through their systems, my size advantage makes no difference. These two are capable of anything and scary as hell. Utterly terrifying when I think of what they might be willing to do to Lacy and our child.

I have to admit, Mama was right—these people need to be handled. Now.

"What kind of deal?" His nostrils flare like a shark scenting baited water.

"The kind you say yes to, no questions asked."

Arlene's bony fingers wrap around Otis's arm as she attempts to gawk at me from behind him. "That don't sound like much of a deal."

"Shut up, woman." He attempts to shake her off, his elbow meeting her ribcage in the process. "The men are talking."

The air whooshes out of her lungs, but it doesn't seem to slow her. A high-pitched whine starts in the back of her throat and quickly turns to an ear-splitting screech. It's an unintelligible sound. And disturbing as fuck.

She launches herself at Otis, her gnarled hands pummeling his arm and shoulder repeatedly.

And he does nothing but continue to stare at me.

God, how did Lacy survive these people? Her brother, Travis, too? She's a fucking superhero, and I'm going to make sure she knows it.

The image of her as I last saw her—windswept hair, kiss-swollen lips, and glowing face—invades my mind, solidifying my shaky conviction. The burning in the pit of my stomach is no longer caused by uncertainty, but righteousness.

This is the right thing to do. For her. For them.

It's the only thing I can do. And I must do *something*. If not, what kind of father would I be? The kind who forces his family to fend for themselves... Sink or swim... Prove their mettle... Just try and beat me at my own fucking game?

Hell, no. I refuse to be that man. I refuse to be like Pa.

"Listen," I tell them both, interrupting the absolute chaos I've inadvertently started. "I'm only going to say this once, and it's not up for negotiation."

Quiet descends upon the scene, both now watching me with those horrid, glazed expressions. But at least they're paying fucking attention. I can only hope my threat reaches whatever's left of their drug-fueled brains.

"Lacy is staying here in Prospect. She's keeping the baby, here in Prospect. Neither of them—not Lacy or the baby— will leave this town. They're with me, and that's how it's going to remain."

Arlene's head bobs along with my words, and my confidence soars.

"And you will stay away from them both. Forever."

"But that's our daughter... Our grandbaby," Arlene says, her voice now small and weak.

Otis, shaking himself out of his silent stupor, pipes in, "The woman's got a point. Plus, your mother already promised us money if we got Lacy out of here."

"Sure, sure." I hold my hands out like a savior bestowing a great gift. "But I'm offering something better. I'm offering you money right now if you promise to leave Lacy and the baby alone. And you can name your price."

Their heads bow together, and they whisper frantically to one another, throwing saucer-eyed glances my way throughout their flurried exchange.

Otis is the first to break from their huddle, shooing Arlene away like a fly. "Any price?"

"Any price," I confirm, holding back the urge to punch him. "But only if you're promising to stay the fuck away."

The blackened smile of victory that stretches his thin lips brings my earlier nausea rushing back. "Deal."

"Yeah, deal," Arlene hollers, bouncing on her toes.

Bile crawls up my throat.

This was too easy. Way too fucking easy. And it makes me sick.

But why?

Money's always been the answer—the key to solving any problem—and I've never thought twice about it. In fact, part of me eats up the ability to get what I want with nothing more than the wave of a few thousand dollars. The power it gives me. The control I have with it. Not much in this world can top it.

Except maybe the feeling I get when I'm with Lacy.

And that, right there, is the fucking problem.

Because I'd do anything for her. Pay any amount of money to keep her and our baby safe. Even if it's the one thing she asked me not to do.

18

───────

LACY

"Uh, honey." Lynette sweeps through the doorway and stops just past the threshold to Oz's office. "I hate to be the one to tell you, but you got trouble."

Her hand perches on her cocked hip, and she arches a brow as if I'm supposed to understand. She didn't say "we" have trouble, but rather *me*, and without fully grasping the meaning, my stomach flip-flops and breaths shorten.

"Trouble?" I push the chair away from the desk and stand.

The quick movement causes a rush of blood to my head, and my vision swims, black dots dancing before me. I sway and reach back for the wall.

She races to my side and grabs my arm. "Easy, there, Lacy. You all right?"

"Yeah." Straightening, I blow a stray lock of hair out of my face and stare at her. "I got up too fast. That's all. You said trouble? What do you mean?"

"Two words." Absentmindedly, she rubs my bicep in what's meant to be a calming gesture, but it only sets me more on edge. "Otis. Arlene."

"Fuck." I slam my fist against the wall. "They're here?"

I'd held my breath through the holidays, expecting my mother and maybe even Otis to come around, but neither Travis nor I heard from them. While it made for a nice Christmas, it was too good to be true.

It's been over two months since Arlene first visited me here, and now Otis is here too. This visit was inevitable and can only mean one thing. They're back to work me some more about leaving town, and while I'm pretty good at figuring out their motives, this one still eludes me.

"Yup. Arlene's pounding them back at the bar and Otis is throwing cash at the girls."

"What?"

Arlene drinking isn't a surprise, but Otis has cash and he's parting with it? What the hell?

All my life, I've watched my parents handle money like water slipping through their fingers. And now Otis is giving it away? That doesn't sound like him at all. He'd sooner part with his wife and kids than give away one red cent for anything other than a fix.

"Yeah, and we're not talking ones and fives either. He's doling out twenties like raindrops and Arlene ain't happy about it. When I left the floor to come get you, poor Gentry was trying to get her to stop screaming like a banshee."

"Goddammit." I stomp out of the office with Lynette on my heels.

When we hit the club, Little Big Town's haunting tune and lyrics of "Girl Crush" strums through the room. Men whoop and holler around the stage where Trixie seductively dances, and from the bar, Roxy glares at me.

She's cleaning up a spill from the looks of things, and Arlene, hanging off one of the stools, looks to be the cause of the mess. I throw an apologetic grimace her way and make a beeline for my mother.

Eyes glassy, Arlene's fixed on the main attraction, expression hard and dark, and as I near, I hear her mutter, "Jackass."

Then with her drink in hand, she lunges to her feet and staggers around the tables and chairs toward the stage. Following her line of sight, I spy Otis to one side of the stage. Just like Lynette said, he proudly tucks several bills under the band of Trixie's hot-pink thong.

"Shit, Lacy, you better stop her. She'll belt him. She's already done it once before." Roxy swings her gaze from Arlene's blazing warpath to scan the club. "Where the hell is Gentry?"

"I got her." I hustle after the drunk woman, but the club's busy with the after work crowd and I'm slow to catch her, weaving around the loud and sociable men.

When I finally grasp Arlene's arm, I'm too late. She's next to her husband, but he's too busy to notice or care. Arlene smacks the back of his head.

Otis bellows, "Motherfucker," and swings his fist in the direction of the hit.

My mother may be sloshed, but she isn't so far gone to

not anticipate his retaliation. She ducks like a boxing pro, and my father's fist connects with my shoulder. The strike knocks me onto my ass. I let out a shocked cry as I hit the floor.

Arlene twirls around, surprised to see me there. Frozen, Otis drops his hand and curses, and at the same time, Lynette, Roxy, and Gentry rush to my side.

"Jesus Christ, Otis." Lynette gets down on her knees beside me. "Lacy, are you okay?" Her gaze drops to my stomach, an unspoken question.

Roxy and Gentry spin on Otis, both grabbing for an arm to hold him still. Although he isn't coming for me--I'm long forgotten—he's still pissed at being restrained.

"I didn't see her, for fuck's sake. Let go of me." He thrashes to get free, and eventually satisfied that he isn't throwing any more punches, Gentry releases him, then Roxy does the same.

Arlene tugs on Lynette's arm, trying to get her to move away from me. "She's all right. Aren't you, honey?"

"Yeah, I'm fine." I take Lynette's hand and let her haul me to my feet.

Suddenly, Roxy's at my side with a glass of water, looking sheepish. "You should probably sit down." She too dips her eyes to my middle.

"I'm fine." I brush at my backside, not wanting to give thought to the filthy floor and what might now be on my jeans.

Taking the glass from Roxy, I splash the water onto my hands and rub them together before drying them on my jeans.

"I'm okay. Can y'all give us a minute?" I glance from Lynette to Roxy and then Gentry.

Reluctantly, they nod and leave me with Arlene and Otis, though we're far from alone. I motion for the two lowlifes that I can't seem to shake to follow me to the office. Otis grumbles profanities and about how he's missing the show, but Arlene drags him along.

I close the door behind us and through clenched teeth and with barely any patience, I ask. "What are you doing here?"

"We came to see our baby girl." Arlene pats at my forehead and I slap her hand away.

"Don't." My fingers tighten on the doorknob. "What the hell are you doing here and throwing around cash? Did you rob a bank or jump someone?"

Every muscle in my body tenses, on edge as I wait for their response. My question isn't a joke even if I wish it were.

Otis guffaws. "Nah. We've come into luck. Got our own fairy godmother." He glances at his wife conspiratorially. "Or I suppose I should say fairy godfather."

She chortles and nods before looking at me, overjoyed. A shiver runs through me and I white-knuckle the knob. The Kincaides.

Otis and Arlene must've finally figured out Ridge is the father. Are they blackmailing his family? Or him?

No, if they confronted him, Ridge would have come to me first. Wouldn't he?

"What are you talking about?" I force my body to relax even if I fail to do the same with my tone. "You can't come in here throwing around cash like that."

"Why not? It's our money. We got it fair and square." He snorts and puffs out his already too big belly that hangs over the waistband of his grubby jeans.

"Yeah. And forget about leaving town." Arlene waves the notion away. "We're staying. We got a better offer."

"A better offer?" I narrow my gaze. "Start talking."

There's so much more going on here, and while I don't know what it is, it's plain to see they got a payout. And now there's no doubt in my mind...it has something to do with my pregnancy.

"Your baby daddy knows how to take care of us." She pulls open her purse to reveal a stack of bills. *Shit, that's a whole lot of money. How much is that?*

Her crooning tone hauls me back to the conversation. "He's gonna be a good father."

Otis snatches a wad from her handbag and smiles while fanning the bills as if to tempt me. The hairs on the back of my neck rise, and nausea swirls in the pit of my stomach.

"Stop beating around the bush. What are you talking about?"

Clearly enjoying themselves, they cackle and grin at each other like cats who ate the canary. I glower and inhale deeply, trying not to give in to the sick desire to strangle them.

He stuffs the cash into his pocket. "Ridge Kincaide gave us money."

At the mention of the one name I'd hoped not to hear, beads of sweat break out at the base of my spine. I swallow with difficulty, trying to keep a hold on things.

"Lots of it." Arlene clutches her purse to her body.

"Why would he do that?" My voice is measured, sounding cool and controlled even to my own ears, although I'm anything but.

He shrugs. "I want another drink."

With a final and dismissive look at me, Otis marches toward the door, and because that's where I stand, it feels like he's charging at me. Hastily, I step to the side, and my shoulder suddenly throbs where he hit me.

"Me too. But Otis, you ain't giving the girls any more." Arlene bolts through the open doorway after him. "You hear me?"

"Shut the fuck up, Arlene."

Our conversation plays in my head as I leave the club to head across town to Canyon Spring Ranch. The drive is a blur, and even as I park and march through the building to Ridge's office, there's only one thought running through my mind. I have to speak to Ridge and get to the bottom of this.

He's on the phone when I barge into his office, but with a look of startled concern, he ends the call immediately.

"Is everything okay?" He gets to his feet and is only inches from me when I raise my hand in the universal sign for stop.

"No, everything isn't okay."

"What is—"

I cut him off. "Why'd you give them money?" and as I ask the question, my arms wrap around my stomach protectively.

His eyes widen but he doesn't ask me who I'm talking about.

Because he knows. He already fucking knows.

"Mama went to them first. She offered them money to get

you out of town." Both his voice and expression are solemn, eyes never wavering from mine. "She and I agreed the only way to fix it was to make them a counteroffer. A better one."

He steps closer and I shake my head, not able to feel his heat or smell him, not when I need to be strong. I step back, and he dips his head on a sigh before continuing.

"I took care of it."

"By giving them money? Real smart, Ridge." My sarcasm cuts deep, making him jerk as I utter his name.

Features tight, he stares at me intently. "What else was I supposed to do?"

"You were supposed to leave it alone. Money doesn't fix everything, and you throwing money at people like Arlene and Otis Hallman is a huge mistake."

"I disagree. The problem is solved."

His smug demeanor pushes me like a bully would the smaller, but not necessarily weaker, kid on the playground. I snort and widen my stance, now realizing what has to be done.

"You didn't solve anything. Only made it worse." I shake away my lingering doubts, the silly part of me that cares for this man and hoped we could have a future together.

I rake a shaky hand through my hair. "My par..." I stop, somewhat stunned at what I was about to say.

Parents.

Why would I even call them that? I hardly think of them as my parents, haven't since I was a little girl. Since I realized Travis is my one and only family. Clearly, he still is.

The pregnancy hormones strike again. With the baby on

the way, I seem to have children, parents, and families on my mind all the time. And I'm more emotional than usual.

Thinking about things I can't change even if I wish I could. Or more importantly, things I wish I had but know can never be. Our gazes lock and something inside my chest cracks. I look away for a blink, needing to wrestle my emotions back behind the locked door.

"They aren't going to leave you alone. You've only invited more trouble. It's like a blackmailer. If you give them money once, they know they've got you. You've got plenty and they will come back for more."

He frowns and studies me in silence. Maybe I've finally gotten through to him. Though Ridge isn't one to easily admit his mistakes, and I'm not surprised when he offers a placating smile, like I'm worrying for nothing. Like he has everything under control.

"If they do come back, I'll set them straight. It was a one-time deal."

An aching sadness pinches at the center of my chest, and I force myself to look at him, even as I'm shaking my head. "This isn't going to work."

"What the hell are you saying?"

"I won't keep you from our baby." I back away from him while maintaining eye contact. He needs to understand I'm serious, no matter how much this hurts.

"Lace—"

Once again, I lift my hand to stop him.

The house. The cute stuffed animals, the adorable night-light, and all the newborn necessities he brought for

Christmas pour over me like fresh cement, sticking me to the spot.

It's as if everything we've dreamed of or done up until this point, all of it is trying to stop me from doing what I must.

What is right.

"Ridge, please. I won't stop you from being in your child's life. I know you'll be a good father. But you and I... We're done."

19

———

RIDGE

I know you'll be a good father.

Lacy's words circle my mind in an endless loop as I arrive at Mack's house. Round and a-fucking-round they've gone for five damn days and six sleepless nights, and I still can't make sense of them.

Hell, I'm such a confused and tired wreck, I can barely remember driving over here. Now that I'm safely parked in the driveway, I take a moment to collect myself.

With a few deep breaths and a quick glance in the mirror, I should be ready to go, but the reflection that stares back at me is shocking.

Red-rimmed eyes. Uncombed hair. Five days' worth of stubble on my face.

What would Mama say if she knew I was showing up on someone's doorstep unannounced, looking like a beggar?

Fuck. Why is it always my mother's voice I hear when

things in my life go sideways? Her terrible advice is half the reason I'm in this mess to begin with.

Pull your shit together, asshole. I'm here to see my friend. I don't need an excuse for that, and I sure as hell don't need to put on a show.

I swipe a hand down my face, shake off the hesitation, and jump out of my truck.

Mack's house is a small brick bungalow, right in the heart of town and only a few blocks from the rental where Lacy and I got frisky. It's nothing like the sprawling ranch he grew up on, and it's about ten times too small for a man of his size. Yet somehow, with its painted shutters, smoking chimney, and lights strung along the eaves, it suits him.

And even though he spends most of his time working at Canyon Spring, and living on-site with our other hands when things are extra busy, this place is warm and welcoming. A home built for a family. Perfect for a guy like Mack, who'll one day make a great dad, I bet.

Not like me. I'm the kind of man who was born to be a bull. Molded to be a relentless sonuvabitch who stops at nothing to get his own way. I've got no ability to compromise or make nice when things don't go according to my plan.

Yeah, I'm a fucking delight, and about the furthest thing from decent dad material as you can get.

Yet, Lacy said those words and she meant them. *I know you'll be a good father.* But how? How the hell could I ever be when it turns out I'm a perfect replica of Pa?

This whole time I've prided myself on being shrewd enough to win the head seat of Canyon Spring and to always stay one step ahead of my competition—no matter who that might be. I thought I was smart enough to win over Lacy this way too.

But the truth is, just like Pa, I've cheated, lied, blackmailed, and tried to solve every problem with money. I demand respect instead of earning it, and act as if I'm king of the damn county. I can't be trusted.

Hell, I couldn't even keep a simple promise to the most important person in my world. And now I've lost her.

Although... *Fuck*... Did I ever have her to begin with?

My mind's too scrambled to sort it out, which is why I'm here. I need a new perspective. A fresh set of eyes to help me figure my shit out. If it's even possible to resolve the chaos I've created.

"Ridge, hey... What are you doing here?" Mack towers over me from inside his foyer, his neck turning a shade of crimson that almost matches his hair.

What the hell is he blushing about?

"Thought I'd come by, drink a beer with my best bud, and catch up, but if it's a bad time..."

"Nah, not a bad time at all." His eyes dart to the adjacent room, just out of my line of sight, and color creeps farther up his face.

Liar. But how fucking odd is that? Mack is many things—mostly, a soft-hearted idiot—but I've never known him to lie. Especially not to me.

"Come on in." He opens the door wider and steps back, gesturing for me to follow. "Was there something on your mind?"

"Actually, yeah..." My words stall as I step into the front hallway and spy Laken through the doorway, sitting on the living room couch. Glancing back over my shoulder, I see her truck parked on the street, right in front of the house.

Christ, I was so caught up in the haze of my own bullshit, I didn't even notice.

As though by reflex, my hand clamps down on Mack's arm, stopping him in his tracks. My teeth grind together, and my blood pressure spikes.

"What the fuck is my sister doing here?"

With a quick flash of his gaze her way again, he shakes his head. "I have no clue. She showed up about thirty minutes ago and has talked my ear off about a horse she wants to buy. I'm not sure why. Maybe she thought you were too busy to consult about it?"

With a deep sigh, I release my stranglehold on his arm and whirl to face my little sister. "Laken!"

She jumps at the boom of my voice, her hands skittering over her lap to smooth down her skirt. When was the last time I saw her in anything other than denim?

"Ridge, hi. How are you?" Her smile is bright, highlighted by the pink lipstick she's wearing, and she bats her tinted lashes at me.

She's wearing makeup. A skirt and fucking makeup. My rough and tumble little sister looks a bit like a pageant queen —polished and sophisticated. She's beautiful. And young. Really fucking young.

What's the worst part of this scene—my sister's obvious attempts to attract my best friend or his complete oblivious-ness to it?

Either way, it's a problem. One I'll need to nip in the bud

before it has a chance to blossom. Hell, the ten-year age gap alone is enough to make Pa roll over in his grave.

And here I am, thinking just like him. Like an asshole. Again.

Fuck.

"I'm not so great right now, Laken. I was hoping for some time with Mack. Alone."

"Oh, sure," she says, standing awkwardly in heeled boots that look way too fancy and are probably borrowed from Scarlett. "I'll get out of your hair. No problem."

"I can help you out with that horse another time, if you'd like," Mack offers, rubbing at the back of his neck, which is still the color of a tomato.

Laken's stride stutters a bit at his words. "That would be great, thanks."

I turn my back on them and walk through the living room, into the kitchen. There's only so much of their polite yet clumsy exchange I can handle. It's too fucking strange, and I'm already at my limit for life-altering events to worry about.

Besides, whatever's going on here is really none of my business. Despite her usual demeanor, Laken's an adult and can make her own decisions. And she could do a hell of a lot worse than Mack–even if he is still pining for his ex.

The fridge is well stocked, and although the beer I'd suggested would be my normal go-to, the thought now somehow turns my stomach. I reach for a bottle of water instead, and it's almost gone by the time Mack joins me.

He seems intent on avoiding eye contact as he grabs a

couple of beers and motions for me to follow him to the backyard. "I need some air."

Silently, I keep pace with his long stride and brush a dusting of snow off the seat he offers me.

We sit, staring into the fenced-off, snow-covered yard, and I listen to some kids playing a few houses over, Lacy's words still running through my head, like backup vocals to their joyous sounds.

"Listen." Mack breaks the uncomfortable tension. "If you don't want me to help her, I won't. I'm not as ignorant as you think, and I know it bothers you."

"I don't want to talk about that right now," I snap, my voice rougher than intended.

"All right. Well, something's clearly on your mind. So why don't you just spill it."

I sigh, and the weight of the past five days pushes down on me, sinking me farther into the chair. My limbs feel like lead, and the ache in my chest threatens to crush me.

Where do I even start?

"I screwed up again, and I don't know how to fix it. Don't know if I should even try. I'm not sure there's any redemption for me this time."

"Did Lacy toss you out on your ass for being a control freak?"

I whip my head to him, my heart banging hard against my ribs. "How the fuck did you know that?"

He shrugs and offers me one of the beers. "With you? It's a given."

"Glad to know I'm so predictable." The winter air chills

my bones but does nothing to ease the fire swirling in my gut.

"So what did you do to sabotage yourself this time?"

Sabotage? The word sounds so foreign. Not because I haven't done a hell of a lot of it in my lifetime, but because the idea that I might be doing it to myself never fucking occurred to me.

"I went behind Lacy's back and gave her folks some cash to stay the hell out of her life. They were going to cause trouble—Mama had already waved a big golden carrot in front of them—and I thought I'd cut them off at the pass."

"So you tried to solve a problem that didn't exist yet by throwing money at it?"

His words echo Lacy almost to the letter. How many times did she tell me the way I used my money was an issue? She told me it was too much. Asked me to tone it down.

Why the hell didn't any of it register?

"Yeah, I guess that's exactly what I did." I finally crack the beer open and take a sip, hoping the alcohol will ease my tension. "She was furious when she found out."

"Aw hell… You really are great at digging yourself those holes." Mack's reaction is to be expected, but it pisses me off anyway.

"What was I supposed to do? I've rehashed the scenario over and over and still don't see another way it could've played out."

Anxious energy courses through me, and I can no longer sit still in this chair. I stand, pacing in front of him as I once again scrutinize my own actions.

"The situation with Arlene and Otis was at a tipping

point. They could've easily become dangerous at any moment," I say, waving my beer at him. "People like them can't be trusted, and someone had to step in. Someone had to shut them down. If not me, then who?"

"I get it." He's way too fucking calm for my liking. "You saw a threat and felt the need to act. But how did Lacy want you to handle it?"

The adrenaline fades, leaving me breathless and a little unsteady on my feet. A light wave of nausea hits as I lumber to my chair, crashing back into it like a deflated balloon.

God, I really did fuck this all up.

"She asked me to leave it alone." The words are bitter ashes on my tongue. "Said she wanted to handle them on her own."

Mack only nods, his gaze still focused on the shoveled pile of snow in front of us.

The sick feeling lingers, but without an obvious remedy, I guzzle back the beer instead. Maybe I can get drunk enough to forget about it. Or maybe the cloud of alcohol will bring an unorthodox solution.

Or maybe I'm just fooling myself and have been all along.

"What if I'm not good enough for them?" The words tumble out—embarrassing and hopeless sounding, yet true. "What if Lacy and the baby are better off without me?"

Mack turns to me now, his brows pinched together and mouth drawn down. "Why would you ever think that?"

"Well, look at what I've done."

"Sure, you can be a cruel son of a bitch when the situation warrants, and you've allowed your mother to influence your decisions a time or two too many." With his shoulders squared and voice firm, Mack's usual teddy bear persona seems a bit more grizzly-like.

"And you're a stubborn jerk most of the time. Maybe all the time. But it's hard to believe you'd ever intentionally harm either one of them."

"Hell no, I wouldn't." He might be my best friend, but he's lucky I don't punch him out for even suggesting such a thing. "All I wanted was to protect them."

He nods again, that damn bobble of his head aggravating as shit. "Because?"

"Why the hell do you think?" *Infuriating bastard.*

"Why don't you just pretend I don't already know the answer and give it to me straight?"

"Because they're the most important people in my life. 'Cause I love them. I love Lacy and a kid I haven't even met yet. And I'd do anything for them. I'd fucking die for them, Mack."

The asshole smiles. "Yeah, man, I know."

"You do?" I choke, not on my admission, but on the overwhelming feeling of purpose it gives me.

"It's obvious. You've been devoted to her from the moment you first uttered her damn name to me. But does she know it?"

My throat tightens further. "I have no idea. I mean...I bought her a house."

"A house doesn't say *I love you.*"

"Maybe you're right. Maybe I should've told her."

"Why didn't you?"

Because I didn't want to give up control. Didn't want to

make myself vulnerable. Didn't want to risk getting hurt and losing it all.

Fuck.

"Okay, so I tell her. But what if it's still too little, too late? How the hell am I going to convince her to take me back?"

"Not sure I can help you with that, my friend. But you'll figure it out. After all, you're a Kincaide and you've got a million resources at your disposal, I'm sure."

A million and a half, at least.

But that's the answer, isn't it?

The weight that's been holding me down is lifted, and suddenly I can breathe. I take a big swig of my remaining beer, relishing both the easy way the frothy liquid slides down my throat and my newfound sense of direction.

"I'm going to give her exactly what she wants."

Mack's brows rise, and his mouth ticks up in a smile. "What's that?"

"The truth, and a choice."

LACY

"I'm gonna fucking kick his ass." Travis takes a long pull on his beer and slams the glass onto the table, causing white foam to bubble over the mouth of the bottle.

"Easy there, cowboy." My fingers curl around his fisted hand. "No one's kicking anyone's ass."

My brother has been in a foul mood ever since I told him what Ridge did. Arlene and Otis flush with cash is only the start of a major, never-ending headache. And while Travis broods, I try not to wallow in my heartbreak.

"Lacy, if I see his smug, pretty-boy face anywhere near you—"

I snag his beer and hold it out of his arm's reach and try to ignore my thundering heart at the thought of coming face-to-face with Ridge. "You'll do nothing."

He snatches the bottle from my grasp. "I'm not promising

anything, but the way I see things, his asshole move finally opened your eyes."

Travis still thinks Ridge's only part in this should be to pay my medical bills and for the baby's expenses.

He can't fathom Ridge has any other use and doesn't know what a good father looks like. Why should he? The only thing Otis Hallman has ever been good at is getting high.

I sigh and roll my eyes, not wanting to argue with him about anything, least of all Ridge. While I stack our lunch baskets and move them to the side of the table, my brother tips his head back and nearly finishes the beer in one gulp.

He wipes his mouth with the back of his hand. "At least one good thing came out of all this."

My brow arches and my lips quirk, curious what he thinks the silver lining is.

"You don't have to be hitched to the likes of Ridge Kincaide anymore. Good riddance. You don't need him."

My lips press together to stop silly words, fed by my even sillier heart, from springing out of my mouth. Travis has it all wrong, but I can't possibly tell him that I do need Ridge, and maybe more importantly, all I want is Ridge.

More than a week has passed since I last saw him, even though he's called and left several messages. After the first message, which I made the mistake of listening to, I now delete them all and refuse to pick up the phone when it's him.

His message only tore at my heart. He was a wreck, drunk even, and maybe more shattered than I am. But I can't think about him. About how the end of us is hurting us both.

We're through.

Done.

We have to be.

"While we are no longer together, we'll be forever connected by the baby." My hand rubs my belly, and I can't help but smile, even if it hurts to think about the future I'd briefly envisioned with Ridge going up in smoke.

"Fuck, don't remind me." Travis hangs his head for a second.

Here I thought things might finally change. Building a life with Ridge might finally rid me of the Hallman stigma. But Ridge is out, and Arlene and Otis are spending like the end of days is near.

By now, most of the town of Prospect is aware of where the money came from. The gossip mill is running strong and steady. And boy, oh boy, did we give them something to talk about.

Doesn't help that dear old Mom and Dad never could keep their mouths shut, especially if they think they have reason to gloat. Those idiots think they got one over on the Kincaides.

And dammit, they aren't wrong.

As far as they see it, I'm their eternal, winning lottery ticket.

And as if Travis can read my mind, his question cuts through my disparaging thoughts. "What are we going to do about Arlene and Otis?"

The sick, sinking feeling that now lives in the pit of my stomach whenever I think about them boils and scorches its way up my throat.

"Don't you mean how are we going to stop them for asking for more money as soon as they burn through whatever outrageous amount Ridge gave them?" Hand shaking, I lift the glass of water to my mouth.

"You two all right?" Kelly sidles up to the table to take our lunch baskets.

It isn't her job, but she's been sticking close to me since things fell apart with Ridge, and I'm grateful for her support.

Travis nods and hands her his bottle, hanging on to her hand longer than is necessary. Kel flushes and mumbles she'll see me later as she spins toward the kitchen.

I watch my brother eye my best friend for a beat or two. He thinks his interest in her is unnoticed, and if I called him on it, he'd deny it or remind me of all the ways in which Kelly is wrong for him.

He catches me looking at him, and his jaw tightens as he scans the club. While it's open, only a handful of customers take up the dark corners of the room, drinking alone or waiting for their favorite dancer to come out and offer a lap dance.

Eventually, his gaze swings back to mine. "Fuck, Lacy, maybe this is it."

His dark hair sticks up in all directions from the countless times he's run his hand through it, and his warm brown eyes are steely, locked on mine.

I cock my head to one side and worry my bottom lip. "What are you talking about?"

Is he going to fess up to having feelings for Kelly or is he still talking about Ridge?

He leans forward and grabs my hands in his, squeezing tight. "Let's leave town."

Like a flag riding up the flagpole, my spine straightens. "What?"

"Look, we both know our shit parents are going to come back for more. They'll hound you and me. Make a whole lot of trouble. But they can't do that if we aren't here."

I've been living with Travis since breaking things off with Ridge, and once or twice, we've joked about skipping town, finally getting out of this place, but he can't be serious.

"Of course they can." I pull my hands from his grip. "It doesn't matter if we're gone, they'll go back to Ridge. Make his life a living hell."

"Yeah, exactly. It'll be his problem, not ours." He shrugs and slides back into his chair. "And it would serve him right."

My insides churn. A part of me likes the idea of leaving Prospect—it was always an option and something I'd planned on doing before the baby. But it feels wrong to leave Ridge to fend off Arlene and Otis.

"I don't know. It doesn't seem right."

It would be like throwing Ridge to the wolves. Though some might say he could handle them. The man's as scary as a charging bull when he wants to be. But it might take a lot of trial and error before he figures out how best to deal with Arlene and Otis, and he'd be sure to have scars when all is said and done.

And why is this my problem? He's the one who created this mess.

"Fuck right." Travis snorts. "If he cared about what was

right, he would've talked to you before going to our fucking parents. Or better yet, he would've kept his nose out of it."

Exhaling a long, exhausted breath, I rake my fingers through my unruly hair. "I don't know."

"What's holding you back?"

It feels wrong, like I'd be running away, but maybe that's my silly heart talking again. It certainly would be easier to live someplace not too far so Ridge could see the baby, like Helena or even Winslow Grove—any place that isn't here. Any place where I wouldn't risk running into him all the time. A place where I wouldn't have to watch him move on and build a life with someone else.

"Maybe you're right."

"Of course I'm right." He slaps his palm on the table. "We could start new, and Arlene and Otis wouldn't be our problem. Listen, I've gotta get back to work, but what do you say about us continuing this conversation over dinner?"

I force a smile, uncertain if we're doing the right thing but not willing to sit by and let everyone else around me move forward.

"Sounds good. Kel's giving me a ride home. You okay if she has dinner with us? I'm not keeping this from her and I'm not going too far from Prospect. I plan to see her often."

He stands and shakes his head then wordlessly nods and leaves.

I power off the computer just as there's a knock at the office door. The day is done, but my mind is still running the mental list of everything I need to do. It's been three days of non-stop conversation and planning with Travis, but I'm finally ready to leave Prospect.

"Come in," I holler, slinging my purse over my shoulder, and stop dead in my tracks at the man standing in the doorway.

Hat in hand, in a blue cotton button-down and dark blue jeans, Mackenzie Mitchell smiles warmly at me before awkwardly clearing his throat. "Hi, Lacy. It's nice to see you."

Cautiously, he ambles into the office, and despite his polite manners and gentle gaze, I cross my arms over my chest.

I can't help but be defensive. He may not be a Kincaide, but he's Ridge's best friend. And as if that wasn't enough cause to distrust him, he also works for the vipers at Canyon Spring Ranch. Heck, he's practically one of them.

"Mack." Instinctively, I step back behind the desk, seeking some kind of physical barrier between us. "What can I do for you?"

"I promise not to take up too much of your time, but I wanted to have a word with you."

"About what?"

He scratches at the back of his neck and clears his throat once more. I don't know this man, but if I was a gambling woman, I'd say he's nervous.

"Before you tell me where to go, I've gotta say that I know it isn't my place to stick my nose in your business."

He doesn't have to say another word. I know this is about Ridge. My body tenses, and as though he picks up on this, he leans back against the wall to give me more space.

"But that's what you're here to do, isn't it?"

Mack isn't someone I know well, or at all really. Over the years, I've seen him around town and often with Ridge. For that alone, I want to tell him to get out. Who cares if I'm rude?

But here's the thing... Anyone who has ever spoken about Mack has only ever had good things to say. Even Oz speaks highly of him, says Mack is a kind and respectful sort. Because of that, out of my love and trust for Oz, I lower my shoulders and try to give this man the time he's asking for.

Ridge hasn't said much about his best friend, only to speak about him in vague terms. Though, from the little he did say, he cares deeply for him. I'd even venture to say he loves him like a brother. The kind of brother he may never have had with the ones he has through blood.

"Yes." His sheepish smile doesn't soften me one bit, though it's a battle to keep myself shuttered against this man's seemingly genuine intent. "Before I get started, I want you to know Ridge didn't ask me to come here and plead his case."

If not for my rib cage, my heart would be out of my chest, leaping at the mention of the man I'm trying in vain to forget.

"He told you about us? About what recently happened?" I don't want to say too much in case Mack doesn't know.

He's right; this isn't his business.

"He told me some. Enough for me to get the idea that he made a grave mistake and you two are no longer together."

His pause is long and again, I wish I knew Mack better because this feels deliberate, like he wants me to say more. Maybe enough to hang myself?

"And?" I push, suddenly hot and claustrophobic in this office.

"I've never seen Ridge like this before. He's a mean, stubborn, son of a bitch, and though not the right thing to say, I mean that quite literally."

A bark of laughter erupts from me, and I quickly slap my hand over my mouth. Not embarrassed at liking his insult of Sage, but more shocked at how easily he's put me at ease.

I grin. "You'll hear no argument from me."

"I didn't think so and I can't say I blame you." His fingers dance along the rim of his hat. "Like I said, I've never seen Ridge this...raw and vulnerable." Now it's his turn to laugh. "He'd punch me if he could hear me now."

"Okay, so we're both in agreement that he can be an asshole but there's another side to him. But why are you here?"

His expression sobers. "If he's as important to you as I hope he is, you need to know that he's changed for the better. Or more to the point, I think you've brought out the best of him."

I open my mouth to shut him down, but as if sensing this, he holds up his hand to silence me.

"He made a mistake, despite trying to protect and take care of you. And you may not have wanted that—I get it. But all of this is new to him and he's learning as he goes. That isn't an excuse, and it doesn't let him off the hook...I know this. I think deep down, he does too."

His bushy red eyebrows draw together, and he meets my gaze head-on. "But Lacy, you need to be honest with him too. He needs to understand what you want and how to be a better partner. How to give up some of that damn control."

The smile he gives me is genuine, and I want to trust what he's saying. I want nothing more than to believe. "Also," he continues, "I think you should know... You and your baby are the most important things to him. Nothing else matters."

I gasp, almost uncertain I misheard him. "Ridge told you that?"

"Yes, and then some." He glances down to the tips of his well-worn cowboy boots before lifting his head to capture my gaze once more. "I guess all this is to say, I'm here to ask you to give him a second chance or at the very least, hear him out."

21

LACY

"Lacy, come on." Travis's nostrils flare and we stare at each other from across his tiny living room. "You can't waffle now. You told me that you were done with that asshole."

Since I called things off with Ridge, we've been talking about how and when to leave Prospect. We even decided where we'd like to go. Well, that was until Mack's visit two days ago.

My brother doesn't know about my conversation with Mack or how I am thinking about giving Ridge a second chance. Though he's quickly putting it together since he only just mentioned setting a moving date and I faltered. I threw at him a million different reasons why now isn't a good time to make a move.

"Shit. We agreed to leave. I even went to Winslow Grove yesterday."

At the mention of the smaller town about forty minutes away, where we'd agreed to settle, my stomach sours.

I purse my lips to keep from throwing up. "You did?"

"Yeah. I talked to Eddie." Travis beams, eyes shining. "He plans on winding down his time working, and he wants me to run the garage. I'd kinda be my own boss."

If Oz is like a father to me, Eddie Winslow is the closest thing to a father figure in Travis's eyes. While they live in different towns, Travis spent all his summers during high school working in Winslow Grove at Eddie's garage. He's the reason why Travis wanted to be a mechanic and own his own garage.

"Oh, T..." I'm both thrilled at his news and sick with guilt. How am I going to tell him that I've changed my mind? "I'm so sorry, but I'm not sure if leaving is the right thing to do."

I grab my coat and scarf from the couch, not wanting to cut the conversation short but also aware that Oz is expecting me. "The responsible thing to do would be to try and work things out with Ridge...for the baby's sake."

"What the fuck did that asshole say to you to make you change your mind?" He narrows his gaze. "Did you forget about how controlling he is? How he meddles in our business? Gave Arlene and Otis money?"

With every reminder of why Ridge and I aren't a good idea, why I moved out in the first place and broke things off, my head throbs.

I can't look Travis in the eye. He has a point. But I meant what I said. I owe it to my child to come to some sort of understanding with its father. Ridge and I might not end up together, but we could be civil, live in the same town, and raise our child together. Or am I being foolish?

"No, I haven't forgotten." I rub my forehead. "Travis, it sounds like leaving might be right for you."

The idea of Travis moving away doesn't sit well with me, but what kind of sister would I be to hold him back?

"Jesus fucking Christ." Fingers threaded in his hair, he growls, "Lacy, the Kincaides will bleed you dry." He grabs his keys from the table, throws on his jacket, and swings open his apartment door. "Fuck, I need to get out of here, but I'm not leaving town without you. If you aren't going then neither am I."

"Travis," I call after him, but he slams the door before I can say any more.

ॐ

Both my conversations with Mack and Travis race through my mind on my way over to Oz's home. Travis was supposed to drive me, but when he stormed out, I had to call a taxi.

And since there's only two in town, I had plenty of time to rehash recent events, over and over again while I waited for my ride.

Oz contacted me first thing this morning, and while I don't work weekends, I figured that's why he texted. Instead, he invited me for lunch.

It's not that unusual for us to have a meal together, but given the timing, I'm guessing the invite has something to do with Ridge. Oz knows I'm living with Travis. No doubt he knows a heck of a lot more than I've told him.

When I get to his small bungalow, there are two vehicles in the driveway—his truck and an all too familiar shiny black SUV. It's one of the Kincaides.

Before I have a chance to guess which one of them it belongs to, Sage Kincaide parades out Oz's front door. She's in a long fur coat, black leather boots with easily a two-inch heel, and no surprise, her makeup and hair are perfect.

Her steps stutter when her gaze lands on me at the end of the walk, but the crack in her flawless veneer is so quick, so insignificant, that I wonder if I imagined it.

She raises her chin and makes a face, features twisting like she's stepped in dog shit, before she wordlessly brushes past me.

It's as if I'm not there and in turn, not willing to bat an eyelash or worse, let her see my confusion, I amble toward the door.

My fist's poised to knock when Sage says, "Lacy."

Foolishly, I glance her way and immediately regret it when I spot her annoying sneer.

"It's a pity you didn't slow down on the weight gain." She's shaking her head from side to side and glares. "You're carrying a lot more than just baby."

Before I can even consider lobbing an insult of my own, she slips into the car and slams it shut.

Oz opens the door and grabs my arm to pull me inside. "Lacy, get in here."

"What the hell is she doing here?" Steaming mad, I whip

off my scarf, gloves, and coat, leaving them in a heap on the bench in his front entrance.

He smirks at my ire, but his expression quickly shifts into something more serious that matches his voice. "She showed up about fifteen minutes ago. Uninvited."

"What did she want?"

"Hang on, before we get into that. What do you want first, the good news—which is the reason I asked you over—or the bad news?"

"I'm not going to be able to focus until I hear why she was here."

"All right. She came to talk about you." He hands me a glass of water and I drink it in one gulp, not realizing how hot and bothered that woman makes me. "Listen, before anything, you need to settle down. This can't be good for the baby."

Oz leads the way into his living room, and I narrow my eyes on him. "The baby is fine and so am I. Tell me what she said."

He places his hands on his hips, jaw firm, and gives it to me straight. "She wants me to fire you." My mouth gapes open and I struggle to find the words, but he isn't finished. "Or more like, she came to deliver a message from Ridge. He doesn't want you working at my club."

"Oh no, he didn't." A red-hot flash blazes a path from my chest to my face.

I spin on my heel, heading for the door with only one thought—give Ridge Kincaide a piece of my mind.

Oz tugs on my arm, carefully spins me around, and guides me to the couch. "Um, Lacy, you gotta calm down." He sits next to me. "Sage was all too happy to deliver the message, and even threatened me if I didn't fire you."

"What the hell?" I grab his weathered hand and squeeze. "Oz, I don't want to cause you any trouble. I'll quit. Consider Friday my last day."

"Wait a sec. While I appreciate your concern, you're not quitting. I need you." His fingers tighten around mine. "Besides, I gave her a message of my own for that son of hers."

He pauses to make sure he has my full attention, and a slow smile pulls at the corners of his mouth. "He can go fuck himself. No one threatens me or any one of my staff. For as long as I'm breathing, Lacy, you'll have a job." He pinches the tip of my chin and holds my stare. "You got me?"

Tears prick at the corners of my eyes, and I nod, unable to speak. Why would Ridge do this?

Though he never wanted me working at a strip club, I thought he understood what Oz and the rest of them meant to me. If this is his way of getting my attention, or worse, to make me dependent on him, he's got another think coming.

"Look, honey, I don't know what happened between you two that has you now living with Travis." He holds up a hand the instant that I open my mouth. "And I don't want to know. All you need concern yourself with is this little one." He points to my mushrooming stomach. "No one is going to hurt me or put me out of business. Trust me. Now, are you ready for the good news?"

He gets to his feet, not waiting for my response, and slides a large, covered item out from behind the couch. His hand grips the blanket and casts it aside, revealing a wooden baby's bed.

"It's a pendulum cradle or some call it a bassinet. For the baby." He chuckles nervously. "I made it from hickory and stained it this dark red mahogany."

"Oh, Oz, I love it." My fingers shake as I run my hand along the smooth railing on one side. "It's perfect."

"I figured for the first little bit you'll need the baby close at night. You can put this next to your bed. And if the baby fusses, you can lie in bed and do this." He gently swings the bed from side to side.

I push onto the tips of my toes and slide my arms around him. "Thank you so much." I kiss his cheek and he flushes.

"Glad you like it." He pats my hand. "Don't let this crap with Sage and Ridge get to you. I understand it's hard, but focus on the good things." I follow his gaze to the cradle that's so much more than a gift.

His gift is something I can pass down to future generations, and in many ways, it feels like the first real mark of the family I'm creating and what will be our traditions and memories.

Although, at the mention of Ridge, the urge to cry doubles. He could have been a part of that. Part of my family. My world. But now, I'm not so sure.

Not even an hour ago, I was stupidly considering giving him a second chance. What the hell is my problem?

22

RIDGE

*E*ach step is filled with purpose as I race up the stairs leading to Travis's apartment. It's still hard to stomach the idea of Lacy living with her brother instead of me—even if it is my own damn fault.

Still, my sense of determination has never been higher. Even when I was stealing the ranch's head seat out from under Brooks's nose, I didn't have this same fire.

Then again, nothing's ever been this important, not even Canyon Spring.

By the time I reach the landing, I'm winded, my body shaking from not only the exertion but the anticipation of what I'm about to do, and the possibility of how Lacy will respond.

There's no time to waste, yet I still hesitate before knocking.

What if she refuses? What if I'm too late? What if I've already lost them?

With my heart ready to pound its way out of my chest, I rap my knuckles on the cheap and dingy aluminum-clad wood, ignoring the voice in my head telling me to bust in like I own the place.

It's difficult and unnatural for me, but I shake off the idea that I'm the one in charge here, because I'm not. Everything from this moment forward is up to Lacy.

I rub at the pain behind my breastbone, and the breath catches in my lungs as the door swings open.

She stands at the threshold, hair cascading over her sumptuous breasts, cheeks flush, and eyes sparkling with what looks like a mix of lust and fury. It's only been a bit over a week, but the swell of her pregnant belly looks impossibly larger, as does the scowl etched on her glowing face.

Christ, she's beautiful.

No. She's so much more than that. She's fucking devastating. And she holds the key to my heart—my entire being—in the palm of her hands. Does she know that?

One way or another, she's about to find out.

"Ridge." My name sounds like a curse on her lips.

Is that good or bad?

Fuck, why am I so nervous? "Hey, Lace. Can I come in? I need to talk with you."

She glowers at me, the pool of her dark eyes eating at my soul, but she doesn't budge.

"It's important," I rush out, ready to beg if that's what it takes. "And it's for the baby, but if now's not a good time, just tell me when."

Without responding, she turns and walks toward the

living room, leaving me to guess at her intentions, but at least she didn't slam the door in my face.

Before she has a chance to change her mind, I hurry after her, kicking the door closed behind me. My long stride easily cuts the distance between us, but I stop short when I see Travis lounging on the couch, rubbing at his stomach like he's the one who's pregnant—a mess of plates and empty meal containers scattered across the coffee table in front of him.

"Shit, did I interrupt your dinner?" I ask, suddenly feeling impetuous and out of place. Why didn't I look at a clock before barging in?

"It's fine. We're finished, aren't we, Travis?" Hands on her hips, she gives her brother a knowing look.

His answering huff indicates otherwise, but he sits forward, gathering up the dishes, and mumbles, "I'm gonna finish something, all right."

"Leave the mess," Lacy says with a smirk. "Ridge can clean it up for us."

A spark lights inside of me. God, this woman is something else—something wonderful and magnetic—and I'd be falling head over heels if I wasn't already completely gone for her.

"No problem." I give her my most charming smile, and more sparks ignite as her gaze collides with mine, eyes wide and mouth agape.

She's so goddamn sexy and she doesn't even know it. The way she stares, hands fidgeting at her sides. The way she catches herself ogling and tries in vain to look away, running her tongue across her bottom lip.

Fuck, every little innocent move makes me want to grab her and kiss her until we're both gasping for air. Until she's wet, panting, and ready to plead for mercy. Until there's nothing left between us except our growing child.

But we're not alone, and despite how good physical contact would be—or how loud my body screams for it—it's not enough to solve this problem.

I clear my throat, forcing my libido under control and my mind back to the task at hand. "Travis, I'm glad you're here, since this impacts you as well."

His brow wrinkles, and he eyes me with suspicion, but he doesn't say a word. Abandoning the dishes, he eases back into his spot on the couch.

Lacy follows suit, and with a heaved sigh, sags into the chair behind her, props her feet on the corner of the table, and absently runs a hand over her stomach. The touch seems second nature, yet it holds such tenderness, I'm momentarily caught up in the simple beauty of it.

Desire of a different sort courses through me, and I stand before them with the energy of my singular goal driving me on. I'm a man on a mission with my stance wide, jaw squared, and mind set.

Yet, Lacy frowns, seemingly unmoved by my show of conviction, and my insides are now churning. Those sparks of hope, lust, confidence, are all dampened by the absolute dread that, from out of nowhere, swamps my system.

"I'm an asshole." I shrug, not afraid of admitting what they both already know. "A rich asshole, and I'm used to getting what I want."

I don't miss the roll of Travis's eyes, but it's Lacy's reaction

I'm concerned with. She seems intent on my words, helping to further my resolve and allowing me to push past any lingering doubts.

"Not saying it's right," I continue, clenching my fists at my sides. "But I've never thought twice about using my family's power, influence, and money in my own self-interest. It's how I was raised. Both my folks taught me this through example and direction. It never crossed my mind that there was another way of doing things."

"We already know firsthand how your family operates." Travis still looks calm, but there's no mistaking the harsh edge to his voice. "Money talks. We get it. Now, get to the fucking point."

A lump forms in my throat. His dislike of me is no secret and never has been. I couldn't say I cared all that much before, but now...fuck, now I want nothing more than to prove to him I'm worthy. Worthy of his sister. Worthy to be called Dad by his nephew or niece. Worthy to be part of his family.

How fucking ironic is that?

Who'd have ever expected a Kincaide to be the one worried about fitting in or being good enough? Especially for a Hallman.

I bow my head in what I hope is a sign of humility. Although, I'm not sure I get it right since it's a foreign fucking feeling and neither of them acknowledge it. "I've never given you a reason to like or trust me, Travis, but I want to change that. I'm willing to do whatever it takes to earn that from you."

His brows draw together, and I sense he's still not buying

what I'm selling, but that's okay. Actions speak louder than words, and right now, all I've got is a promise. It'll take time to win him over. Time I'm hoping to spend.

I refocus on Lacy—the woman who keeps my world turning and is no doubt better than I deserve. "I'm going to repeat that because I mean it. *Whatever* it fucking takes."

Her gaze doesn't waver but neither does the stoic expression she's wearing.

Has anything I've said made an impact? Does she understand the lengths I'm willing to go?

She sighs, shifting in her seat, and a look of discomfort flits across her beautiful features.

Fuck. Of course none of my words have registered. I haven't said anything of value. Nothing of true significance. How can she understand my meaning when I haven't said it plain and clear?

Unable to take another moment of her impassive silence, I rush to her side, my legs shaking from the magnitude of this moment. It's like I'm standing at the edge of a cliff with nowhere left to go.

Her face tilts up, her irresistible gaze drawing me further in.

I take the leap.

"I love you, Lacy," I say, dropping to my knees in front of her.

Her mouth opens on a gasp, and I take her hand, lacing our fingers together over the swell of her belly.

"I love you, and I can't walk away without letting you know how much."

"Ridge." Tears swim in her eyes, and her luscious lips pull downward as she subtly shakes her head.

But I'm not ready to concede defeat. Not when there's important things left to say. Not if there's any hope left at all. And *god*, I'm still holding so much hope.

"You need to understand, I never thought I could have this. My whole life's been dictated from the time I was old enough to remember. Being a Kincaide might seem glamorous and carefree, but the expectations..."

I swallow hard, nearly choking on the words I need to say. Words I didn't see coming until this minute. Feelings that, while always there under the surface, I've been too stubborn and maybe too afraid to admit.

But the only thing left to fear is losing the woman in front of me. "Well, I don't give a fuck about those expectations anymore. Nothing is more important to me than this—than you and our child. And I'll do whatever it takes. Whatever you want."

Her teeth sink into her plump bottom lip, and my dick perks up in notice. The timing is all wrong, but my body has a mind of its own when it comes to her.

Still. the frown she's wearing, and the fact that she won't look me in the eye, has my insides churning. "Whatever it takes? Does that include trying to get me fired from my job?"

The shock from her words almost lands me on my ass, but I grasp her hand tighter, not allowing her to pull away. "You've known from day one I'm not the biggest fan of your job, but you made it clear, and I understand it's important to you. So, I'm really not sure what you're talking about."

"Really?" Her eyes narrow on me but then suddenly flare wide. "Unless... Oh shit... Unless..."

"Lacy?" Travis is sitting forward in his seat again, this time wearing a look of concern.

Her eyes flit to her brother and back to me, her mouth hanging open in a sexy sort of way that makes me want to grab hold and kiss her.

"Lace?" I prompt.

"You didn't ask your mother to talk to Oz, did you?"

Now it's pure and simple rage that's rolling the contents of my gut.

Mama. Fuck, I knew her feigned cooperation was too good to be true. I should have guessed she wouldn't just roll over.

"I'm a bossy son of a bitch, and have made some bad choices, but I've never lied to you. I promise, I had nothing to do with it."

A small smile tips her lips, yet her chin wobbles and new tears glisten in her eyes. "I should have known."

Relief floods my system, and I surge forward to kiss her, but she puts a hand up to stop me.

"That doesn't change anything between us," she says, shaking her head again. "I can't live like this—constantly worrying what your mother will do next to try and ruin our lives."

"Me neither," I admit. "Which is why I have a plan to deal with her."

Finally, she leans toward me, and I see a glimmer of hope. "How?"

"When I said I was willing to do whatever it takes, I meant it." I squeeze her hand. "I'm going to prove it to you, Lace. Trust me."

23

RIDGE

"Well, well... Look who's all here." Mama strolls into my office like there's not a care in the world. This, despite the fact she wasn't expecting anyone to be here but me.

Most of my siblings line the room, making it feel almost claustrophobic. As my gaze sweeps across them, my sense of conviction grows, and I smile at our preening mother.

"Ridge, Trey, Scarlett and Jett, Cole, Brooks. So nice to see you all." She lists our names like she's tallying up the odds. Or taking a mental note for future retribution.

Still, the haughty look of near boredom on her face would lead most to believe she's above us all, fearless and unruffled.

But I know the truth. The fine lines around her tight lips and the way she needlessly fusses with her clothes and hair are dead giveaways. She's at a disadvantage, and she knows it. She's nervous. Scared even.

Good. It's about damn time the tables were turned.

"If we're having another family meeting, then we're missing two." Her smug expression doesn't falter, but her eyes bounce wildly around the room, perhaps assessing who will be her ally in the battle she must sense is coming.

Or is this war we're about to wage?

A few of my siblings shift uncomfortably, and most avoid meeting her gaze. Trey's the exception, but his stoic expression gives nothing away. I hope like hell including him wasn't a mistake.

If he's still grappling with any misplaced sense of loyalty, he could bring this whole thing down. But what other choice do I have? I've got to trust that even though he's helped Mama conceal a whole lot of shit in the past, he'll keep his word. Hell, maybe he'll do it because of that—all the dishonest subterfuge she's asked of him.

Because despite his faithfulness to her—a woman who's as cunning as she is despicable—I think he might be the most honorable one of us all.

"It's not a family meeting." I motion for her to take a seat, but my attention diverts to Lacy, looking a bit shell-shocked as she hovers in the doorway.

God, she's more stunning every time I see her. Will I ever get over that feeling?

Fuck, if this meeting doesn't go right, I might not have her in my life long enough to find out. And from the look on her face, we're not off to a good start.

Still, she's here. She doesn't know the details of my plan or that I've corralled most of my siblings into it with me. I can only imagine what she's thinking, walking into a room full of

Kincaides, including Mama. But I asked her to trust me, and she hasn't walked away yet.

"It's okay," I tell her. "I saved a seat for you."

She seems to come to a decision and, with no further hesitation, comes to sit in the chair beside me.

"As I was saying," I continue, redirecting my focus to Mama. "This is business."

"Business?" She scoffs, turning her sights on Lacy before returning to me. "Then why the audience?"

I clench my jaw, barely suppressing the verbal lashing I'm tempted to deliver. She'd deserve it. That and a helluva lot more. But the subtle shake of Lacy's head catches my attention, urging me to hold my tongue.

Her hands are folded as though cradling our child, her wild hair shines like a damn diamond, and the expression she wears is resolute. She's a picture of pure beauty. Glowing fucking perfection. And no matter what Mama or anyone else has to say, if Lacy wants to be, she's with me.

That's all that matters.

Fueled by this knowledge, I relax onto the chair behind my desk and give Mama an easy smile. "There are no outsiders here. The operation of Canyon Spring Ranch, and the potential of its future success, affects us all. So, everyone's going to be involved in this conversation—as much or as little as they choose."

"What the hell are you going on about?" Despite the perpetual stick up her ass, she somehow stiffens even further, sitting at the edge of her chair.

"Pa's will was clear," I say, ignoring her question for now. "I'm in charge, with the stipulation of marriage–"

"And you've failed spectacularly in that regard," she interrupts. "I went to the trouble of securing you a decent match. All you had to do was follow through. But no, you can't even do that right."

Her sneer is full of contempt, yet there's a desperation to it. It's only a hint, but it's still clear how hard she's grasping. "You treated poor Chastity like garbage, tossing her away on a whim."

"Let's not get carried away. Chastity was a prop you tried to force on me, only I was polite enough to cut her loose. She didn't want me. Hell, I don't think she even liked me. And I sure as shit wasn't going to dishonor her or the woman I love."

I gesture at Lacy, making it clear she's the one I mean. The only one for me. "Especially not based on *your* whims, Mama."

The air around her seems to vibrate with fury. Snarling like a rabid animal, she snaps, "You've been given one too many chances. Now it's my call."

I hum my agreement. "Yes, it would seem you're holding all the cards in this game."

My siblings all look on, engrossed in the building drama. Cole, Jett, and Scarlett each wear a look of anticipation—eagerness, even. Brooks's fists are tight at his sides, and Trey... well, I still can't get a read on him, but he doesn't look particularly happy.

In the chair next to me, Lacy's expression is hard to read. Still guarded. Still gorgeous. And completely unsure of what's happening.

Better than nothing, and at least she's still here.

"Then again." I'm ready to call Mama's bluff. "You've never played a clean game, have you? You've always had an unfair advantage with all your family's money at your disposal and your ability to lie and cheat your way out of every situation. And you've used us, your children, to carry on that legacy."

Her mouth drops open, perhaps to deny or argue, but I won't allow her time to speak. Her tainted words are no longer welcome here. "But you forget, Mama, over the years, you've made most of us an accomplice in at least one of your schemes. I'd harbor a guess that, combined, we know all your dirty little secrets. All those terrible things you want to keep buried."

Now she looks worried. Her eyes grow wide, and she shifts in her seat to look around the room at her brood, stopping when she reaches Brooks. "You promised me."

"Did I?" He shrugs, the tension he's been holding seeming to loosen with the gesture. "You know, I was under such duress at the time, I'm not sure I can recall..."

"Stop it!" Her hand slams the arm of her chair. "You promised me, and you know it."

"Don't worry," I say, calling her attention back to me. "Brooks has kept your confidence. He'll continue to do so, as will I. We all will."

I glance around the room, hoping no one disagrees. "For now."

Trey clears his throat, and although he hasn't budged from his spot in the corner, the faint crease of his brow is a good indication of his growing discomfort.

Shit, I can't let him screw this up. "As you've pointed out, according to Pa's will, you're the one in charge. It's your call as to who gets to run the ranch, Mama. I'm asking you..."

I swallow back a sudden bout of apprehension, and in my silent panic, seek out the dark pool of Lacy's gaze. It pulls me in, settling my nerves and lighting a fire within me. She gives me strength. Fuck, this woman gives me life—even if she has no idea what I'm about to do.

With renewed confidence, I look back to Mama. "No. We're *all* asking you to make that call. The only woman I want in my life is Lacy, and since we know you won't agree to that match, the marriage clause won't be fulfilled. So, it's up to you. We want you to name Pa's successor. Right now."

Hands gripping the arms of her chair, she shakes her head. "You think you can blackmail me into getting what you want? Do you really think I'll name you?"

"No," I say through a growing smile. "And I was prepared to walk away, still am if that's what it takes, but no, Mama... You're going to name us *all*."

"What?" The color seems to drain from her face, perhaps the reality of her situation sinking in. "What kind of game are you playing?"

"Isn't it obvious?" Trey interjects, pushing off the wall to come stand at her side. "Ridge wants us to drive you out."

Mama's eyes narrow on me, and my gut seizes.

"That's not—" Jett starts but is interrupted by Scarlett, who agrees, "Not at all."

Brooks shares a look with Cole before meeting my gaze, his expression full of remorse.

Fucking hell.

They're all going to back out on me, aren't they? So

much for family bonds and blood being thicker than water, or any of that other bullshit. Then again, the way I've treated most of them—not bothered by who I stepped on while making my way to the top—is it any wonder?

Hell, I deserve whatever's coming to me, and if I'm the one who gets pushed out... Well, I guess so be it.

A firm touch smooths over my shoulders, lending me strength and comfort, and I look up to find Lacy standing at my side. Right where she belongs. Where I hope like hell I can keep her for fucking ever, no matter the outcome with Canyon Spring.

"Is that true, Ridge?" Mama taunts. "You're trying to oust me?"

Trey beats me to the punch. "It's true."

His cold stare cuts through me, but I refuse to look away. Refuse to go down without a fight. Because despite not needing control of the ranch or any of it to survive, I still fucking want it. It's part of me, and I'm afraid it always will be.

But maybe it's a part of us all. Maybe Trey's way of protecting it is different from mine. Or maybe his moral compass isn't as true as I'd hoped.

"Ridge wants you out of the business." He's as uncompromising as ever. "And we all support him in that."

It knocks the wind from me. Not only the sentiment of his endorsement but the unexpected hint of emotion, swimming in his gaze.

Never in my life have I been so happy to be wrong.

My chest expands on a deep, satisfied breath, and

continues expanding as Scarlett steps forward with Jett on her heels. "Yes, we do."

Cole follows along. "Sure as hell do."

Mama sputters as a look of sheer terror takes hold of her. With both hands, she latches onto Trey's arm, clawing and pleading, "You can't. It's my call. The will—"

"Can be contested," Brooks says, his tone making it clear we're not messing around. "And have no doubt, if you give us any pushback on this, we will contest."

"Don't even think about trying to use Jasper or Laken as pawns, either." Trey leans toward her, his voice eerily low. "I won't allow it."

Her mouth opens and closes a few times, the shock seeming to take hold. "After everything I've done for you."

My heart almost aches for her—for all the hardships I've seen her through, despite the terrible ways in which she's managed them.

But that feeling's only an echo.

Nothing she says or does from here could make me fall back to our old patterns. I'll never be her pawn or puppet again.

I'm a new man. My own goddamn man.

And I've got the prospect of a bright future standing at my side. I just hope like hell Lacy's willing to give me the chance.

The room goes silent as everyone watches and waits for Sage to make her next move. But she only sits there, smoothing invisible wrinkles from her dress, with her head bent and brow furrowed.

Up until now I've been a spectator. Make that a stunned spectator. Is Ridge serious? Is he willing to give this all up if his mother doesn't agree to their terms?

He told me he loved me, and as much as I wanted to hear those words—believe them—I was skeptical. Even coming here today, I was unsure if he knows how to love unconditionally, without strings attached for him to control.

But this feels real—in his penetrating gaze and the unwavering conviction in his words.

All of this feels real. He loves me. He loves our baby. How can I not give him another chance?

Driven to help him, and also never one to sit quietly, I'm overcome with the urge to try and reach Sage. While we aren't friendly and likely never will be, we do have a few things in common.

For starters, there's Ridge's and my unborn child. As much as I don't like the thought of it, she will be this baby's grandmother. Family. And there's still this tremendous and awe-inspiring thing called motherhood.

My baby isn't here yet, but I've had months to realize that this child will tip my life on its head. He or she already has, and my love for this child is unlike anything I've ever experienced before.

A child changes you. Makes you stronger and weaker, and maybe that isn't a bad thing.

"This must be hard." At the sound of my voice, Sage stills her agitated fussing, but refuses to look at me. I inhale and gather all the conviction I can muster. "To feel like your children are turning against you."

Ridge wraps an arm around my waist, pulling me closer, and I squeeze back reassuringly. He must be wondering if any of this has made an impact on me. Did he get through to me? I want him to know that I am with him.

"I haven't even held my child yet, but it would break my heart to think I'd wronged them so deeply that they'd want to push me away."

Sage turns to Ridge and me, her glassy stare landing on the swell of my stomach, and a silent tear rolls down her cheek. A strange ache, call it compassion, pinches at my chest. I figured she was coldhearted, but she's crying. I'm surprised she's capable of such emotion.

Her vulnerability spurs me on, fueling my desire to reach

her. Our baby's future depends on it, and I'll do anything, even bare my soul in front of the Kincaides.

"But it's not too late. Trust me. My parents are two of the rottenest people you'll ever meet, and I cut ties with them long ago. Yet deep down, I still care. They're my family and always will be. It would take a lot, but if they made an honest effort, I'd forgive them."

My voice wavers. Still, I won't let the choke of emotion stop me. "It isn't too late to make things right, Sage. You have a chance to make that effort. Just do what your children are asking. Do the right thing."

Everyone stares at me with varying degrees of over-whelm, wonder, and perhaps even kindness. Scarlett links an arm with her twin while wiping tears from her eyes, and he pulls her close, kissing the top of her head.

Brooks wears a grin that spreads from ear to ear as does Cole. Even Trey's usual frown has disappeared, replaced by a softer expression, and call me crazy, it might even be approval.

For the first time, it feels as if the Kincaides are accepting me, maybe even seeing me as one of them. I shudder, awestruck and also a little freaked out.

"Fine." Sage sniffs and nods, seemingly unbothered by the single trail of wetness, already drying on her face. "I'll contact the lawyer, Charlie, this week to see when he might have time to discuss it. There will be a process to follow, I'm sure. It won't happen overnight."

Does she mean it? Or is this another stall tactic? A way for her to keep the wolves at bay while she regroups and thinks of another plan of attack.

Ridge pulls open a drawer and holds out papers. "No need."

Smiling, he places the neat stack of pages on the desk in front of her. "The documentation is already drawn up—in triplicate, and with page flags to mark the spots where you need to sign. Charlie had no problem doing it right away. He was quite agreeable to it, actually."

She stares, dumbfounded, and I press my lips together to stifle my shock. Ridge isn't kidding. He took the steps to make this happen, and not just someday, but now.

I stare at him with what I'm sure is disbelief or adoration or maybe a little of both, and he winks at me, grinning from ear to ear.

"Lace, you want to hand Mama that pen?"

"Uh." I clear my throat, still stunned by how things are unfolding, and also warmed by his heated gaze.

Without a care for who's in the room or the situation, Ridge only has eyes for me. His need ever-present and growing.

A ragged, lusty breath rushes from me and my cheeks flush. This man has no shame. His naughty grin widens as if to suggest he's well aware of what he's doing to me.

Our fingers brush as I take the pen from him, and I force a steady, "Of course," extending the pen to Sage.

I watch as she signs over the future of Canyon Spring Ranch. Ridge's warm hand lands on my shoulder and gently squeezes.

A small part of me can't help but feel for Sage Kincaide. She isn't a kind woman, but she recently lost her husband. She must still be grieving and now she's losing control of the ranch. It can't be easy to surrender, even if it's the right thing to do, especially for a woman like her.

Before the ink's done drying on the page, she stands, raises her chin in the air like any prideful person would, and leaves the room.

No one follows her—not even Trey. They all gather round, sharing a few hugs and handshakes, and gawk at her signature like they're checking to make sure it's real.

"Well, we did it. We won." Ridge chuckles nervously as if he too can't quite believe it's true.

"No." Brooks sighs, satisfied but resigned. "This is just the beginning. There'll be repercussions. There always are."

"Speaking of repercussions." Ridge glances at me, and I don't miss the subtle tic to his jaw. "We still have another problem."

At first, I'm unsure what he means, then it hits me as he says grimly, "There's also the matter of Lacy's parents."

Jett's brow furrows. "What about them?"

With eyes on me, I fill them in on first Sage's offer and then Ridge's, and end by saying, "Now that they've had a taste of the Kincaide money, they'll come back for more."

"Just cut 'em off." Jett shrugs, clearly missing the point.

Trey curtly shakes his head and looks at me. "We'll make them listen. Understand that leaving you alone is best for them. But for now, let's at least celebrate today's victory. And Lacy, you won us this round."

Startled by the praise, I'm unprepared when Ridge pulls me onto his lap. "Yes, she did. She's an unstoppable fucking force of nature."

I let out a squeak and wrap my arms around his neck. My

lips graze the shell of his ear as I lean in so only he can hear. "You sure you don't want to stop me?"

"Hell no, I don't." His hand threads through my hair, and desire crackles like a live wire between us. "I'm always going to look after you, but I promise, I'll never stand in your way again."

Ridge repositions me with a groan and I squirm over his hardening cock, suddenly remembering his siblings. I glance around the room, cheeks reddening, only to discover they've gone, having closed the door behind them.

"We're alone," I state the obvious and Ridge chuckles, bringing my attention back to him.

"I meant what I said about walking away from it all. I'm still willing if that's what you want." His expression steals my breath—his heart is out, and mine for the taking.

He frowns and—maybe misinterpreting my silence for doubt—rushes on, "I will leave Canyon Spring in the hands of my brothers and sisters, if that's what you want. We can leave it behind, go somewhere new, and forget it even exists. We can start over. You, me, the baby, and Travis too, if he wants."

"You... You..." I shake my head, eyes now brimming with unshed tears. "Why would you do that?"

He smiles tenderly and brushes the wetness from my cheek. "Because I don't want it, Lace. Not as much as I want you. And none of it is worth a damn if I can't have you here by my side."

"I want you too."

His wide, sexy grin causes a flutter deep in my belly, and

a low growl rips from him as he hoists me up onto his desk. With his free arm, he clears the tabletop in one quick sweep.

I gasp as a laptop, papers, pens, and who knows what else clatters to the carpet. "Ridge. You're going to break something."

He looms over me, head dipping toward the crook of my neck. "I don't fucking care. All I care about is you. Being inside you. What do you say, Lace?"

He sucks my pulse at the hollow between my neck and shoulder, and my heart stutters. I'm lost to the feel of his warm, soft lips as he trails tiny kisses down my neck. His teeth scrape at my flesh, and I jerk at the sharp sensation shooting to my core.

He moans against my skin. "Lace, answer me."

Reluctant to focus on anything but what this man does to me, I pull back. "What?"

"I want to make love to you." His hands latch on to my heavy, aching breasts.

"Ridge. Yes." My head falls back onto the desk as I thrust my chest farther into his strong, capable fingers, rubbing the swollen peaks through my flannel.

"We need this shirt off you. All of it. Now." Distractedly, his hungry gaze slides from my chest up to my face. "I'm going to tie your wrists together with your wet panties." He pulls at the waist band of my leggings. "Use these and your shirt to tie your legs."

"Oh God." My thighs rub together with an aching need.

He's right, just the anticipation of him has me wet and burning all at the same time.

I fumble to get naked, needing him inside me, on top of me, all around me. "Let me do it."

Quickly, I discard my clothes and he silently watches, hands fisted at his sides. I can feel the restraint it's costing him to do nothing. To wait. The muscles in his forearms bunch and twitch as he flexes his hands open and closed.

What's even sexier is watching him snap and lose all control. His nostrils flare as his hands dart out, snatching my underwear and leggings from my grasp. At the same time, his mouth closes over my now bare breast, tongue hot and wet, and sharp tingles shoot through me.

I buck and mewl when his thick knuckles brush along my center and he pushes me back onto the desk.

Bared to him, the sight brings a flare of heat to Ridge's eyes, and I shiver at his desire. All of me.

My tongue darts out to wet my bottom lip and honestly, to tease him some more. I love watching him come undone. I've missed him.

Missed this.

Missed us.

"Fuck, Lace. You're so ready." His long digits slide through my slick folds. "Soaking for me."

"I am." I nod and spread my legs wider. The pads of his fingers brush against my sex in a way that sends a pleasurable jolt through me. "Ridge, fuck me."

He bends down to kiss me, our mouths melding, tongues tangling, as he nestles his broad body in the cradle of my thighs. Kissing me, never stopping for air, he unbuckles his belt, unfastens the button, and drops his pants.

His hard, thick cock slaps against my inner thigh, and I

whimper, arousal building low in my core. He lines up his engorged crown with my entrance and pushes inside of me.

My eyes flutter closed on a sob as sensations zip through my body, setting me on fire. My fingers tremble as I dig them into his hair and roll my pelvis to match his deep, fast strokes.

"Lace, you're fucking perfect."

My desperate cries of "deeper," "more," and "yes," wash over me, urging him on. It doesn't take long for my muscles to tense, body strung tight, as my orgasm ripples through me. Almost at the same time, a shudder rolls through Ridge's defined frame and he comes with me.

Both of us covered in a sheen of sweat and sex, and panting, Ridge takes me in his arms and moves us over to the couch.

Once settled, he curls his body around mine and intently stares down at me. "I mean it, Lace, whatever it takes." His fingers intertwine with mine. "There's nothing more important to me than the two of you."

Under our joined hands, our baby gives an answering kick, and suddenly I'm the one dabbing at the tears on his handsome face.

"Amazing, isn't it?" One hand cups his stubbled jaw.

"You're amazing," he chokes out. "So fucking amazing, and I couldn't be more in love with you."

A single tear falls from the corner of my eye. "I love you too. So much."

25

RIDGE

"Everything's looking good." Doc Anderson looks up from between Lacy's thighs with a bright smile and pats her knee. "Won't be long now."

If he weren't her doctor and seventy-something I might be getting territorial, but the soft glint in his eye is more akin to a proud father addressing his daughter. It's the way I imagine I might be looking at my own child soon.

"Thanks, Doc." Despite the good news, Lacy frowns–something she's been doing a lot of lately.

Although, I can't say I blame her. The last month of her pregnancy has been spent on bed rest, yet her blood pressure is still too high. Doc thought it would be best to induce labor, and she's been more than stressed since receiving that news.

Only, our little bundle has decided not to wait another day for that scheduled procedure. Lacy's water broke on its own last night, and we've been at the hospital in Helena ever since.

Still, I can't help but worry there's more to her anguished looks than simple discomfort.

As the doctor leaves, I squeeze her hand, knowing we won't be alone for long. "You're doing amazing."

"I'm not doing anything," she quips. "I'm not allowed."

"I know it hasn't been easy for you, but just think...once you've had the baby you'll be allowed to get out of this bed."

The look she gives me is priceless–genuine disbelief mixed with an air of *I'd like to murder you*–and I do my best not to laugh. Her exasperation is damn adorable.

"Can I get you anything?" I ask, brushing my lips over her temple.

She shifts, winding a hand around my neck. "Just this," she murmurs, bringing our mouths in line.

Our kiss is sweet but brief, interrupted by her sharp inhale as another contraction takes hold. Now she's the one squeezing my hand, and I'm left feeling a bit helpless as I try to soothe her through the pain.

A nurse breezes into the room to check the monitors. "How are we doing?"

Lacy's look of death is redirected. "Just great," she huffs through gritted teeth.

"What about you, Dad? You holding up alright?" The nurse gives me a genuine smile, but I don't return it. There's too much tension in the air, and too good a chance Lacy will hand me my balls if I look like I'm enjoying myself while she's in pain.

But honestly, how could I be anything other than fantastic? I've got a gorgeous woman who, despite her current, completely understandable hostility, is the best damn thing that's ever happened to me. And she's about to deliver my baby. I'm going to be a dad.

I'm going to be a dad.

The room spins a little as I rush to catch my breath. "All good."

"Ridge," Lacy interrupts my mini panic attack, her hand loosening in mine now that the contraction has subsided. "Can you double-check the waiting room?"

"For?"

Another frown pulls her beautiful lips into a tight line, and a deep crease furrows her brow. "I don't know. For anything...or anyone...surprising."

Ah shit. I should've guessed.

Despite not having seen or heard from her parents since my blunder in giving them money, Lacy's still waiting for the other shoe to drop.

Now would be the opportune time for them to resurface, but something tells me it's not going to happen. They aren't just being quiet. Hell, I'm not sure either of them is capable of that. No. They're gone—their trailer home empty for at least a month now, with no sightings of them from anyone in town.

I honestly have no idea where they've gone or why, but I'm not concerned since whatever or whoever drove them off did us a giant favor. Sure as hell did a better job than I did with my misplaced attempts at bribery.

Still, with the Hallmans' track record being what it is, it's smart not to take any chances.

"I'll go check." I kiss her forehead once more.

The waiting area is at the opposite end of the hall, so it

gives me a clear view of all the people coming and going, and there's no sign of Otis or Arlene. In fact, other than a nurse or two, there isn't a single face I recognize. Until I round the corner to the lounge where I find Travis as well as Brooks and Addie.

Travis, wide-eyed and animated, jumps from his seat. "Is it here? Am I an uncle?"

"Not yet, but Doc says soon." I attempt a smile, but anxiety makes it feel more like a grimace. "Thanks for coming."

"We wouldn't miss it." Addie squeezes close to Brooks, as though urging his agreement.

He nods. "Happy to be here."

I'm no fool. Brooks and I will likely never be friends. Not after all the years of my torment. Still, it's nice to think we've moved past the hard feelings and my attempts to be a controlling prick. We may not be friends, but we can be *friendly*. And it turns out we make a pretty good team when we put our differences aside. And other than Trey's unexpected support, Brooks was my biggest ally in getting Mama out of the ranch business, after all.

"It's just you three?" It's still early, I guess, but I'd expected—fuck, I'd *hoped*—more of my family might show up.

At least my siblings. As for Mama... Well, I won't hold my breath. She's done a damn fine job of avoiding me since we took over ranch operations. Since we gave her a taste of her own medicine. I wish I could say her reaction surprised me, but the woman still hasn't learned how to deal with hurt feelings.

"Kelly's here somewhere." Travis rolls his eyes. "Said something about finding herself a doctor. I swear, that woman's a walking fuck—"

A nurse peeks her head into the room, catching my attention. "Mr. Kincaide? Your wife's asking for you."

Without pausing to correct her—because although there's a diamond engagement band in my pocket, I still haven't officially asked Lacy to marry me—or to hear the rest of Travis's opinion on Kelly, I race out of the room and back to my woman.

After five intense, scary, and miraculous hours of labor, Lacy and I welcome our daughter to the world. She's a tiny ball of screaming, wrinkled fury. And the most beautiful thing I've ever seen.

When her writhing body is placed in Lacy's arms, my little girl calms, nuzzling into the warmth of her mother's skin. My heart fucking melts, and then reforms into something new. Something bigger and better.

Because this... There are no words to account for the way this feels. It's complex, all-encompassing, fucking terrifying, and goddamn wonderful all at the same time.

"I love you," I murmur into Lacy's sweat-soaked hair, and run a finger over the back of our daughter's tiny hand. "I love both of you. So, so much."

God, I'm the luckiest bastard in the world. I've got everything I've ever wanted—more than I ever knew I wanted. It's like fate saw me headed down a path leading to self-destruction and decided to step in to save me. And I couldn't be more grateful.

What started as a hitch in my plan turned into this—the best moment of my fucking life.

"She's perfect," Lacy whispers as a steady stream of tears rolls down her face. "Isn't she perfect?"

I hum my agreement, cuddling closer to the two of them, and the rest of the world fades away. Time slows and stops while I stare into the face of the miracle we've created, the beautiful little soul we're responsible for. The highlight of my life. Both of them.

"Am I interrupting?" Mama stands in the doorway, body turned as though ready to leave.

Part of me whispers that I should let her go. Let her suffer just a little longer. She's earned it, after all. But fuck, she's still my mother, and despite her many, many flaws, I've got to believe she didn't intend to hurt me. Or any of her children.

Would it be rational to withhold access to her grandchild? Or just plain-old vindictive?

"Sage." Lacy beats me to the punch, and I hold my breath, waiting to hear the verdict. "Come meet your granddaughter."

"It's a girl?" Mama practically swoons, and I'm not convinced she's acting.

She swishes into the room, hands clasped under her chin as though in prayer, and fawns over the sweetest baby on the planet. "Does she have a name?"

"Not yet," Lacy says, all smiles. "But I'm sure we'll figure it out soon."

"Don't let Ridge boss his way into a name you don't like. Devlin did that." Despite the difficult topic, Mama's voice is soft, and a smile plays on her lips.

Lacy's eyes grow round. "He did?"

Mama's smile widens, and through a low laugh she says, "Ridge was meant to be named Walker, but Devlin changed it at the last minute. I was too tired to argue."

Lacy's laughter is bright and melodic, and my throat tightens as I watch the wall between two of the most important women in my life begin to crumble. Not that I expect it to come falling down in a single day, and not that I forgive Mama or plan to let her back in any time soon. Hell, that wall may never be eliminated completely, and I might be the one helping to hold it up, but at the very least, this moment has knocked a few bricks out of it.

Travis races into the room like his ass is on fire, the wild energy from earlier back in full force—or maybe it never wore off—but the second his eyes land on my mother, he halts, his back going ramrod straight.

"It's a girl," I tell him, hoping like hell he can play it cool. I'd hate to kick my future brother-in-law out of the room before he gets to meet his niece.

"Trav," Lacy calls, capturing his attention away from my mother. "Get over here."

He comes to the other side of the bed, eyeing Mama warily. She offers him a polite nod, and Travis finally relaxes, bending to murmur sweet nothings in my daughter's ear.

Brooks and Addie are next to arrive, followed by Mack, with Laken trailing not far behind. Their joy for us is clear on their faces—even Brooks's.

As Addie coos over the baby, and Laken so obviously moons over my best friend, Mama puts a hand on my shoulder. "Congratulations," she says. "You deserve to be happy." And with a final tight smile, she leaves.

The relationship will never be what it once was, but that's probably a good thing. This is the start of something new. With some luck, something better. But at the very least, something I can decide the boundaries of.

The rest of my siblings come in on what seems like a rotation. I'm not sure if it's planned or impromptu, but as happy as I am to have them all here with us, it's nice not to have everyone in this claustrophobic-feeling hospital room all at once.

By the time they've all had a chance to offer their congratulations and ogle the beauty of our precious child, Lacy's worn out. She's a trooper and won't admit it, but I can see it in the droop of her shoulders and the slow dip of her eyelids.

The baby starts fussing, her tiny mewl of hungry anger reminding me a lot of her mother.

"Okay." I stand, ushering the stragglers out. "No one's going to get a free show here. Lacy's going to nurse the baby, so y'all need to leave. Now."

Cole chuckles at my antics—like he isn't the kind of perv who'd try to cop a peek—and Scarlett drags him out with a huge smile on her face, but Trey lingers at the door, motioning for me to join him in the hall.

"What's up?" What's so important that he'd drag me away from my woman and new baby only hours after birth?

"Just wanted to set your mind at ease." His eyes dart to the room behind me, and he drops his voice to a near whisper. "They aren't coming back."

Despite the unbreakable cloud of joy I'm riding, a chill runs up my spine. "Who?"

"Her parents. The troublemakers."

"Oh? And how would you know that?" But even as I'm asking the question, I realize, I don't want to know.

Trey is many things—most of all a fucking mystery—and after the way he handled Mama... *Yeah, I really don't want to know.*

"Don't worry, I took care of it. Now you just need to go take care of them." He nods back toward Lacy and the baby before leaving me with a knowing smirk.

No need to tell me twice.

"Everything okay?" Lacy asks when I return to her side— the place I don't plan on straying far from ever again.

"Everything's perfect." I stroke down her arm that cradles our daughter, who's fallen asleep at Lacy's breast.

Her tired smile fades. "Well, it's not perfect."

My gut seizes, and I move to wrap an arm around her shoulders, ready to protect her however I can. "What's wrong?"

On a heavy sigh, she says, "For so long, Travis and Kelly have been my only true family. Sure, Oz and the rest of them at the club are an extended one, though fleeting and not entirely mine. But this, the three of us, is something alto-gether different."

Her voice wobbles, and I hold back my own tears while trying to decipher how any of what she's saying is bad. I know she's not second-guessing our relationship, which could only mean she's been hurt in some way.

"I know we haven't picked a name for her yet." She dips

her chin to our sleeping angel. "But when we fill out that birth certificate, I already know she's going to have your last name."

"Lace." My voice is hoarse, the clog of emotion near to choking. "I don't understand the problem."

Eyes swimming with tears and voice full of fire, she says, "I'm the only one who's not a Kincaide."

A smile cracks my lips and I exhale through a laugh. "That's only a problem for as long as you want it to be."

"Really?"

"Are you dropping a hint, or is this your way of asking me to marry you?"

Despite her obvious exhaustion, her gaze turns ferocious. "You're supposed to ask me."

God, she's spectacular when she gets feisty.

"Fuck, Lace... I've wanted to make you mine from the moment I met you. All I've wanted is to drag you to the altar."

"Then? Why haven't you asked?"

The smile curving my lips is as genuine as it is devious. "Because I haven't figured out a way that doesn't sound like a demand. And I'm not sure your brother won't try to kill me when he finds out."

She laughs and our daughter stirs, stretching her tiny hand over the curve of Lacy's bare breast.

Distracted by the miracle we've created, and despite the diamond digging into my thigh through my pocket, the subject of marriage is dropped.

At least, for now.

I will ask her when the time is right. Not because of obligation, or expectations, or even because she wants me to. It will be an act of giving—a show of my devotion.

Because as much as she and our child are mine...I'm also *theirs*.

Thank you for reading The Cowboy Hitch. Next in the Canyon Spring universe is Laken Kincaide's story, The Cowboy Crush, a small town unrequited age gap romance.

Thank you for reading and please leave a review on your favorite book site, including tell a friend. Reviews help readers find books!

ABOUT THE AUTHORS

S.M. WEST

USA TODAY bestselling and award winning author, S.M. West writes sexy, angsty stories about brave hearts and wild love, including, more times than not, heart-pumping twists and turns.

Apart from her infinite love of books, she's a self-professed wine, chocolate, and travel junkie. When not writing or hanging with her family, she's usually talking to her characters (in her head) or planning her next adventure.

www.smwestauthor.com

KIMBERLY QUINN

Kimberly Quinn is a steamy contemporary romance author, born procrastinator, and grumpy hero lover. She enjoys lively conversations, usually with imaginary people, and can often be found daydreaming at work.

Her stories are set in adventurous small towns, filled with

beautifully flawed, relatable characters, and have lots of
heart, spice, and sometimes, a suspenseful twist.

When she's not busy writing, she can be found with a coffee
in hand, dog at her side, and exploring the wilds of her
hometown in Ontario, Canada... Or on her couch, getting
lost in a good story.

www.kimberlyquinnbooks.com